The Tree House

Glenn Haybittle

CHEYNE
WALK

Published by Cheyne Walk 2018

Published by Cheyne Walk
www.cheynewalk.co

ISBN- 13: 978-0-9932863-2-2

And now listen carefully. You in others - this is your soul. This is what you are. This is what your consciousness has breathed and lived on and enjoyed throughout your life - your soul, your immortality, your life in others. And what now? You have always been in others and you will remain in others. And what does it matter to you if later on that is called your memory? This will be you - the you that enters the future and becomes a part of it.

Boris Pasternak

Dance is the hidden language of the soul.

Martha Graham

If there is any substitute for love, it is memory.

Joseph Brodsky

1 Who Will Look After My Things When I Die?

There was a mannequin standing at the centre of my grandfather's overgrown garden, a life-size male with black hair and hopeful blue eyes. He was dressed in a black suit, a white shirt and black shoes. The elements and birds had reduced him and his clothes to a forlorn forsaken state. The fine black hair streaked with bird excrement, the cloth of the suit tattered and blanched where the weather had attacked it, the white shirt mapped by colour-quenched stains. Nearby, on the grass carpeted with clover, was a rusted bucket full to the brim with rainwater.

'His expression never changes,' my grandfather said. 'No matter what he endures. I like that about him.'

'I don't get it,' I said.

'He's there just in case Ada is looking down at me and my life. I imagine he would make her smile,' he said and he smiled sheepishly at me, a smile that called to mind a small boy in short trousers with scabs on his knees rather than an adult who had reached retirement age.

'Who's Ada?'

'She's who I invited you here to talk about.'

'Okay,' I said. I was greatly impressed by my grandfather's appearance. A pair of braces hung loose from his striped black and grey trousers, as if he was enjoying a relaxed moment after fruitful exertion. He had a full head of white hair. The striking bone structure of his face, his bones generally caught the eye more than his skin, was no less apparent now than it had been in his younger days. His coppery skin had a manly glow. Genetically, at face value, I had nothing to fear from him.

He led me on up the garden path where grass had seeded between the cracked stones. Before ringing his front door bell I had been reminded of the magnetic pull exerted on me as a child by the aura of an uninhabited house near my home. How persuasively it convinced me of the reality of the supernatural, as if ghosts and magic required the prohibition of lawnmowers, vacuum cleaners, air fresheners and polish to thrive. The house in which my grandfather lived had barely any furniture. The floorboards were bare, splintered and felted with dust. There were no carpets or curtains or chairs. The cavernous rooms relayed echoes back and forth like coded messages to an unseen recipient. No wall, evidently, had received a fresh coat of paint for decades. I noticed an exposed tangle of electrical wires sprouting from one wall through which audibly hummed fitful current. Only the kitchen showed signs of habitation, a rudimentary kind of compromise to convention. He offered no explanations. He had hurried me through out into the back garden.

The garden path eventually vanished into a thicket of massed jungle foliage. My grandfather battled his way through it and I followed. It had been raining and drops showered over me as I fought my way through the clinging tendrils and leaves. Hidden behind was a garden shed draped in wisteria. He had to push at the warped wooden door which groaned and only opened with reluctance. Inside there was a mattress on the floor, a chair, teetering piles of books stacked against three walls and a tapestry of ancient spider webs hanging like safety nets from every cornice and corner of the ceiling. There were two pears and some cheese on a map of Paris spread open on the desk. Dead leaves and the silver paper and torn cellophane from cigarette packets carpeted the floor.

'You live in here?' I asked.

'I'm not a great fan of home comforts,' he said. In the smile and look he gave me I could sense he was trying to gauge how crazy, on a score of one to ten, I thought he was.

There were torn scraps of brown paper pinned to the walls with elegant script handwritten in silver ink. On each was a list.

The blue pinstriped trousers with the cigarette burn on the left thigh = sitting on the shingle at Brighton beach when I was sure I would have to kill myself.

The grey corduroy jacket = my first meeting with Guru at the cult and producing from the inside pocket two thousand pounds in grubby banknotes.

'I'm afraid of forgetting,' he explained. 'Why don't you sit down?'

I sat down on an old wooden sea chest with black iron handles.

'When you hear my story you might think I'd welcome dementia. But nothing alarms me more. I live in the past. If I lose the past I'll be homeless. So I make memory lists. One day I might try to remember as many items of individual clothing I've worn in my life as I can. For example, underpants. How many pairs of the various underpants you've worn through the years can you remember now? Once you remember a distinctive pair, a memory will begin developing in your mind. Things you'd lost start turning up. I like to call this the discipline of the archaeologist in me. Another day I might try to remember all the times I've been to the sea or walked out into snow. Of course probably less than 1% of experience is recorded. As if 99% of our life happens off camera, off stage. You should try it.' An expression of doubt returned to my grandfather's face every time, which was often, he tried to laugh it away.

'I will,' I said.

'I'm going to tell you what happened to me during the war and then I want you to do me a favour.'

There was so much agitation in my mind at this juncture of my life that it was difficult for me to pay close attention to the world outside my head. But to be asked to do a favour always got my full attention, set alarm bells ringing in my blood. I hate disappointing people. Which is maybe why I inevitably do. I disappointed a lot more often than I pleased. I braced myself now to disappoint my grandfather.

It occurred to me that we were both under house arrest in

our different ways. He had the reputation for rarely leaving his home. I was often nowadays fighting off the same criticism, usually from within.

'What kind of favour?'

'We'll talk about that later.'

My grandfather lifted himself with some difficulty out of his chair and began to perform an eccentric dance. I noticed his fly was undone. They say there isn't a single gesture a human being can appropriate that is unique, that doesn't feature in the unpublished catalogue of human gestures. But I had never seen anyone perform a choreography of movements like my grandfather now presented to me. He was like a squirrel scrabbling for nuts in a hanging basket just beyond his reach. His movements were a good deal less fluid but I recognised the performance as the ghost of something he did when I was a child. My grandfather couldn't allow more than five minutes to pass by without making you smile. He had no qualms about making a figure of fun of himself as long as he was rewarded with a wide grin, which I was able to give him now. My father, on the other hand, had such a horror of appearing in any way ridiculous that it was as if he wore a uniform throughout my childhood and was under at all times the critical scrutiny of a superior officer. For this reason I always felt more love for my grandfather than for my father.

My grandfather was the black sheep of the family. My only living relative whose life might make an interesting biography, though I had taken little active interest in it. There's still a mark of his volatility on the dining table of my parents' house where he brought down a mug on the maple wood with such force that it left behind its imprint. I worshipped him when I was small. Then he suddenly vanished for five years and when he came back I found my feeling for him had changed. I resented him, secretly made fun of him at every opportunity. I'd never, up to this point, asked myself why. I'd never enquired where he went when he vanished. My parents are both tight-lipped. Personal life to them is like something to be boxed up with the Christmas decorations in the attic. I sometimes think there are essentially two kinds of people – those who take an interest in remembering their dreams and those who don't. My parents fall into the latter category. I knew my grandfather had been cuckolded by my grandmother and I knew he had inherited a lot of money from a virtual stranger under very suspicious circumstances. I knew he had had more than one mental breakdown. There was a story that he had once emerged naked from a changing room in a department store and begun shouting at the top of his voice that he didn't want to buy anything, nothing at all.

'Shall I tell you my memory of you as a child?' he asked me. 'You froze whenever you felt my attention too closely on you. Of course that's the natural response of children to adult interest. The adult is authority's surveillance camera, the child is the guilty keeper of secrets. How old are you now?'

'I'm twenty-eight.'

'And now you're stuck in a rut.'

'Who says I'm stuck in a rut?'

'You live in a halfway house.'

This was true. I lived in a hostel near Tower Bridge. The building itself was like a multi-storey municipal car park with dormitories. There was a dead plant in the reception area that no one ever thought to throw out. My grandfather had called me yesterday. The receptionist had to climb three flights of stairs to knock on my door and inform me there was a telephone call for me. I never received calls at the hostel. I had long since disappointed everyone who might feel an impulse to find out how I was doing. So when I received a phone call I expected news of a death or at the least a serious accident. Instead it was my enigmatic grandfather. To my knowledge it was the first time I had ever spoken to my grandfather on the phone. Certainly the first time I had heard from him in years. He asked me to visit him, on a matter of the utmost urgency. Thus had I walked today from Tower Bridge to his home in Notting Hill.

'When we're stuck in a rut we have to look in the rear view mirror before we can move forwards. It might help you to learn more about your family tree. There's a whole heap of stuff behind us, like compost, which constitutes energy both pushing us on and holding us back. First I'm going to tell you a story of how one moment of stupid vanity can poison the rest of your life. It's easy to say don't do anything you'll be sorry for but sometimes we have no inkling at the time of how sorry we will be. Of course we're all prone to misgivings which send us back on our tracks. But, in my case, it was something much more searing than a misgiving. There's a question I now repeatedly ask myself. Who will look after my things when I die? I've made up my mind it has to be you.'

2 Love Song

'Before Ada and I became friends, I was frightened of the dark. I had a stub of candle and a secret stash of matches hidden by my bed. In bed with the lights out I used to feel the darkness lift me up and float me away until I dissolved into it. I didn't like this feeling. In fact, it terrified me.

'I told Ada about this feeling. I could tell her anything without feeling shame. And she gave me a stone. She said it was her favourite stone and it would stop me floating away. All I had to do was hold it in the dark. One of the most agonising mysteries of my life is how I managed to mislay that stone. I should have guarded it above all else and yet I carelessly lost it. That stone was like our engagement ring. The touch of her hands would have remained a presence on that stone.

'This will be the first time I have ever spoken of Ada to anyone. More than one psychiatrist has tried to wrestle her out of me but I always fought them off.' He struggled to his feet again and mimed how he fought off the psychiatrists. Once again he earned a wide grin from me. 'Psychiatrists are just like everyone else at heart; they think what we most want is to be known, to have all our secrets laid bare. Ever since Ada, the last thing I have wanted is to be known. I wasn't going to give up my silence, not to them, not to anyone. Do you know what the most secret stubbornly-defended part of our identity is? It's the private concessions we make to our cowardice.'

3 A Promise

'First of all you should know that I never knew who my mother was. She gave me up soon after I was born. You didn't even know that, did you? Almost immediately after my birth I was taken to a friend of hers who lived in Paris. Not far from the Shakespeare and Company bookstore in rue de l'Odéon. I wasn't required to call my guardians mama or papa. There was no pretence that they were my real parents. She was Camille; he was Paul. I liked Paul and I especially liked Camille but I was never able to show them much affection. I've no doubt I appeared ungrateful and surly. I couldn't bear to be touched by Camille. I fought her off. The only times I allowed her to touch me without screwing up my face in disgust was when I didn't want to go to school and had to pretend to be ill. Every time she touched me it was as if the possibility of being touched by my real mother diminished. They were childless before I arrived and still childless when they were separated years later. Camille I'd describe as pinched looking, rather brittle and apologetic by nature. She liked to knit. A pastime which made her appear much older than she was. I think it was the accomplishment she was most proud of. The nimble dexterity of her hands. She also liked making pastry, for the same reason. Paul liked to sleek back his hair and roll up his sleeves as if motivating himself for a great effort. I don't though remember him ever exerting himself in any meaningful way. He was in no way suited to times of war.

'I was about nine when I developed a cunning in obtaining information about my mother. Direct questions on my part were always deflected. They also led to attempts on Camille's part to appease me with her hands. It caused Camille pain to not answer my questions – her apologetic nature. But I sensed she had made my mother a promise and she always kept her promises. I could tell she held my mother in very high esteem but perhaps against her better judgement. And that my mother caused a lot of conflict in her. As if she was relentlessly having to give her the benefit of the doubt. So what I did was to draw a picture of a woman with crayons and scrawl the word "mama" underneath it. Then I got up after I had been put to bed, sneaked into their bedroom and placed the picture on their eiderdown and hid beneath the bed. I knew they would talk about my mother when they saw the drawing. Which they did. That way I discovered her name was Elisa. That she was living in Italy. Venice. That she wanted to be a dancer. And that she had been raped. Except, of course, I had no idea what raped meant. The dictionary didn't help much. There seemed to be something fishy about the story she had told Camille and Paul. Paul was critical of her; Camille defended her. I did this a second time a few weeks later and was caught when I sneezed under their bed. But not before I had heard Paul ask where the photograph of Elisa was. Thus I discovered it was hidden beneath Camille's jewellery in a box. The box with its wooden carvings of fronds, petals and winged creatures had always fascinated me. But I was in no hurry to open it. I wanted to prolong the excitement for as long as possible. And the best way to achieve this was to share my excitement with my best friend, Ada. We lived together in a tree house her father had built her in the garden of the house next door. Or we pretended we lived together. We probably spent three hours every day in our secret hideaway. From the age of eight until the age of eleven we were inseparable. When Paris was blacked out for fear of air raids we even made midnight trysts and would creep out into the garden in our night clothes. It was at these times that our naughty games took place.

'Love was a great mystery to us. Probably the biggest and most alluring mystery of all. We talked about it a lot without understanding it was what we felt for each other.'

4 Disintegration

'I was seeing a dancer,' I told my grandfather. In fact I had found it hard to concentrate on what he was saying after he mentioned that his mother wanted to be a dancer. I was sucked back into the broken circuitry of my own recent narrative. There was a second synchronicity too. The unearthing of a synchronicity in our personal life can be exciting. The suggestion that there might be a submerged and mapped order to everything that happens implies that there are depths, layers deep, with far reaching connections and greater freedoms beneath the claustrophobic maze of our life above ground. My dancer, Katie, had once slept among the books at the Shakespeare and Company bookstore. Before I knew her she had spent a week in Paris with three of her fellow dance students. They had tried their hand at street performing and the bookstore owner – his name was George, I think – had let them all sleep in his shop in exchange for helping out behind the counter. It was one of her favourite memories. She had shown me photographs.

It hadn't been an act of vanity which had poisoned my life but rather a stupid decision, made without thinking, which began unstitching every single achievement I had made. Five years previously I had been the singer in a band. There were five of us and we had been friends since school. I was triumphantly proud of my four friends. They provided me with the ideal frame for how I wanted the world to see me. It felt right that we stood on a stage together, picked out by spotlights, where we were able to publicise all the inspiration and exaltation we found in each other's company. Together we created a sound. I loved our sound. How much transfiguring adrenalin it pumped through my body. And on top of that I was going out with Katie. In those days little of importance seemed exterior to myself. I felt as though I was a long way down the path to becoming the polished product of my will, the self I chose to be. We did a gig at Dingwalls in Camden and received a rave review in the NME. At our next gig the audience was full of A&R men from all the major record labels. When we entered public places I would always receive a vivid sense of how charismatically glamorous we were as a group. We all wore makeup, we all dressed with great attention to detail, we all spent a good deal of time in front of mirrors. Katie joked that I spent more time in front of a mirror than she did, which, being a dancer, was of course hours every day. She had just auditioned for Pina Bausch's Tanztheater Wuppertal Company in Germany. I loved watching her dance and I wanted her to succeed in her aspirations as a dancer but I didn't want her to go to Germany, though I found it hard to admit this to myself.

One night I met a notorious and charismatic hard guy of my London neighbourhood. Someone you didn't want to get on the wrong side of. His presence was like an electric fence.

You could sense all the high voltage running through him at arm's length. His name was Jazz. He had heard of my growing fame and I was flattered he took an interest in me. Against my better judgement, I let myself be persuaded to return to his flat. All of a sudden everyone wanted to know me. I had always found it difficult to say no to any request made of me. An imperative of my nature was that I always appeared friendly. I suppose it was the equivalent of my grandfather's idiot dances. Nowadays I'm compelled to almost always say no to all requests made of me. It's a measure of how altered, how strange to myself I've become. Jazz's girlfriend Karen was inside the flat. Karen was one of those girls who can't help miming sexual arousal even when bleaching a sink or counting out coins in a shop. She didn't listen to men; she watched them, for signs of arousal. In the end you had to look at the swell of her breasts. It was like a conjuring trick she performed. She looked like she would have no qualms performing any sexual act asked of her but also like she might stab you with a pair of nail scissors. I did my best not to look at her exposed cleavage in case Jazz noticed but it remained the room's focal point, its magnetic heart. There were lots of pills and day-glo capsules on the glass table. A casualty ward drama was on TV. Someone was being cut open by men in green bibs and plastic bonnets. I didn't bother asking what the two blue pills I swallowed were called or what chemicals they contained. Before long I began seeing patterns of light at the edge of objects. Things looked at acquired an echo as if they were sounds. Things heard exploded into colour. The immediate and known was erupted into by bewildering galactic distances. Then panic, jumping and spitting like a firecracker, entered my mind and wouldn't be extinguished. Panic such as I had never experienced, utterly disproportionate, as if I had suddenly gone blind or was fighting for breath. The sophisticated gainsaying part of my mind had been obliterated, replaced by a primeval darkness from which all kinds of unprecedented likelihoods threatened to take form. It was as if everything I knew about myself was coming to an end.

The next day a menacing fin surfaced in the waters of my mind while I was with Katie on the tube. Clearly one rogue chemical had disrupted all the laws by which my mind created order. It was suddenly as if I was living in a different reality to everyone else. The world seemed to be turning much more quickly, foreground flooded with background, the irrational science of dreams overruling my everyday perception of the world, as if anything might happen next, as if there was far more at stake than circumstance revealed. I felt for the first time in my life I had the deeps of the ocean within me, the darkness of prehistory. It was like I had been flayed of a protective layer of insulation and many of the certainties by which I lived my life had disintegrated. I felt the mounting fear was distorting my features. At any moment I expected to lose every last shred of dignity I had. I might start vomiting, I might start screaming. And I was trapped. There wasn't a door I could open myself and flee. With the realisation that I had no autonomy came panic. My heart thrashed like the heart of a wild hunted animal. The imperative now was to conceal this panic from everyone around me, a panic that whitewashed the faces opposite of all individuality, turning them into the many heads of one awakening monster. My imagination brought the train to a halt in the tunnel. Then it was as if all the air was sucked out of the carriage. My relief when the platform of the next station appeared was immense. It wasn't our station but there was no way I could endure another stretch of the underground tunnel. I forgot about Katie in my desperation to get off. I turned round on the platform to see her looking at me through the greasy glass with bewilderment.

I only had to imagine myself on a tube train to know it was now an experience denied to me. I soon discovered the same thing happened to me on buses and trains. Public transport was now out of bounds. All of a sudden simple things I had always taken for granted, like going to Camden Market with Katie (that reminds me of how much virgin hope we're able to invest in every new item of clothing that takes our fancy), were transformed into nightmares. I had to invent excuses to get out of all the things I was no longer able to do. And I was too ashamed of myself to explain to Katie why. Thus I began to behave irrationally. I insisted on walking everywhere. Katie began to look at me slightly askance. One night I made her walk from Kensington High Street to Chelsea, both there and back. She was offended when I tried to persuade her to get the tube alone. As the next gig loomed I was terrified. I kept thinking, what if I have a panic attack on stage? And, of course, that's exactly what happened. The former euphoria turned to terror. I had to leave the stage before the first song ended. My friends were angry with me. I lied to them. I was too ashamed to admit that something was going horribly wrong in my head. I simply told them my heart wasn't in it anymore. An ad was put in the NME for a new singer. Meanwhile Katie had two pieces of news for me. Tanztheater had accepted her and she was pregnant. She quickly made it clear that there was no question of having the child. However I let slip an idea I should have kept to myself. I was used to speaking my mind with Katie. It was a fundamental part of the intimacy we shared that we allowed each other to say what we were thinking. I told her I sensed that if I didn't have this child I had a feeling I would never have a child. I didn't mean it as any kind of tentative prohibition but she would soon use it against me as an indication of my crude insensitivity. The other problem was, she decided to have the abortion in Oxford where her parents lived. She wanted me there with her. But there was no way for me, in the state I was in, to get to Oxford. Nor could I bring myself to explain to her why.

I could no longer trust my own mind. And my fear of showing fear increased the fear. I could only relax if there was no one near me, no one watching me. Katie sent me a short angry letter which made me realise that I was so caught up in my own dilemma I had viewed the abortion as of little more import than a visit to the dentist. When she came to see me to formally finish our relationship I barely recognised her, so hardened had she become. It was like she had erased all her memories of me, concreted over all the layered archaeology of our relationship. I sensed how much guilt she was suffering but was unable to make her feel any better about her decision. I remember she was continually countering objections I hadn't made. Telling me it was only a cell, not a person, and that millions of fertilised eggs are rejected and how angry she was at the way abortion is viewed, how she had to be labelled as depressed and unable to cope to be eligible and how she felt she was on trial. She told me how alone, how abandoned she had felt in the lift of the clinic. 'Every other girl had a partner there with them,' she told me. She compelled me to experience her loneliness and sense of abandonment. But she treated me with so much scorn that I imagined her scorn would only increase if I admitted the reason I was unable to be with her that day. I couldn't find the words that would make my new terror of public transport sound plausible. On television I watched people on planes and trains with the envy you might regard someone winning an award for the thing they most love doing in life. She wanted no further words from me. She clearly felt there was nothing left of our relationship except that bald patch of turf under a swing. I didn't care about the abortion; I was deeply sorry how much suffering it had caused her and I just wanted to go back to how things were. Pretend the abortion hadn't happened. An insipid and stupidly naive response I realised afterwards.

That was to be the last time I spoke to her. Three days later she left for Germany.

What had happened to me, I realised, was that my social persona, my protective clothing, had been torn from me. I no longer had a double life. I was left with only my private self and felt stripped naked out in the public galleries of the world. Only music and books, occasionally, helped mother me back to the fugitive respite of a more innocent world.

When I felt like a startled wild creature, thoughts no longer connecting, coherency degenerating into hallucination, I channelled all my dwindling resources into trying to hold my head like someone accustomed but indifferent to admiration. The madness in my head I could just about contain as long as no one else perceived it. It reminded me of hiding fear when I was a young boy. As if once you gave someone an idea that was harmful to your self-esteem that idea accumulated a lot more power to damage you. What determines the nature of the next moment is often not how things are on the inside but how they look on the outside. Children know this: act the part of pirate or princess and before long you become the pirate or the princess. For both good and ill we become what people think of us. Therefore no one was to know how difficult it was for me to get through the most straightforward of days. No one was to know how mad I was.

I now experienced the world in terms of boxes. Every moment of every day seemed a box of one kind or another. There were some boxes I could cope with; others I had to avoid at all costs. Even there in my grandfather's shed I was sometimes impatient to return home. Often I forced myself to go out only so as to know the relief of finally returning home. My safeguard today was that I was inside a box I could immediately leave if need arose. This was why I had walked from the east end of London to Notting Hill to meet my grandfather instead of catching the tube. I didn't however tell my grandfather any of this. I was still too ashamed.

5 Your Silent Face

'I can't remember what Ada looked like anymore,' my grandfather said. He lifted his liver-spotted and bone-ridged hands to his forehead, as though trying to massage away a headache. 'If I try to summon her it's like she's enveloped in smoke. I get a glimpse of the texture of her hair, her white socks and sandals but her features have been erased. Why can I see her sandals more clearly than her face? I can even remember the way she wrote her name in the flyleaf of her school books. I can still see her handwriting but I can't see her face. But I remember the atmosphere of the intimacy we created together as if I only have to say a magic word to feel it wash through me again. I like to think of the intimacy we shared as like that force, whatever it is, that allows spiders to walk on water.

'At times she laughed, continuously and unrestrainedly. Or there were long silences when I was struck by the vulnerability of her veins, the delicacy of her bones, the sudden flares of heat and arousal of which her body was capable. I remember I used to think that she had the sea within her, the rising and falling of waves, the crash of surf, the fountains of spray. Sometimes I could feel the blood coursing through her veins just beneath her skin, the pulse in her breast. I remember the sound of her breathing quickening and the way she sometimes rasped out a faint sighing note of sadness or pleasure.

'I remember once we shared a cigarette.

'I remember, like all children, we had our own private manner of communicating. We invented words and a sign language. We had secret signals when adults constrained us to silence.

'I remember the same things attracted us. Like the prismatic drops on a spider web or the faithfully repeated choreography of a bird that alighted in the garden at the same time each day. Only by startling it could it be made to change its cherished routine.

'Every new day Ada and I became friends afresh. I think this is always the case between true friends. The excitement of each other's company receives a fresh dousing of dew every day. Our excitement in each other's company was such that we couldn't bear anyone else to see it. We could only share our secrets in the privacy of our tree house. Talk for us was always exploration, as if we were entering secret caves, crouched down over remote rock pools, wading out naked into the sea at night.

'Every single item in our tree house had a sacred quality. The simple act of carrying it there ensured this. We were very conscientious about what we brought with us there. It was as if God was always with us in our tree house. Which, at times, was a disturbing sensation. Because, whatever else God might be, he's definitely an adult and adults were our enemy. Even Ada's father, who was one of the nicest men I have ever known, was our enemy.

'Everything we brought up into our tree house was material for our book of spells. Every page was devoted to one particular spell. There would be a drawing – we took in turns to do the drawings; there would be a four line incantation which we always composed together and seven magical objects glued or sown to the page. A piece of tree bark, the filaments of a spider web, the feather of a bird, a strand of coloured wool, a flower seed, a button. Things like that. We had a chemistry set, paints, needles and thread. We had the clothes of Ada's dolls. We also cut off small strips of our own clothes where adults wouldn't notice and pasted them in. We invented a choreography for each spell. I would practice dances in front of the mirror in my room before showing them to Ada. They had to be just right. But there was no way of writing these down so we probably forgot the dance which accompanied each spell. Making up dances was a way for me to bring my mother closer, to ingratiate myself to her.'

'You still make up dances now,' I said.

'I've always found it difficult to turn over a new leaf.' He playfully slapped his cheeks with both hands. Then adjusted the black framed glasses on the bridge of his nose. 'As children we don't often think beyond the moment. This was to be the case with most adults as well during the war and occupation. But our spells were for the future. Not one of these spells did we ever perform. We were saving them up. Ada and I made lots of plans together. We imagined adventures. We imagined going into the sea together, digging in the sand. We imagined leaving our footprints in a field of fresh snow. We imagined sleeping in a tent together. It never occurred to us we might be separated.

'The book became heavy and crisp with all these things stuck to its pages. It was an old ledger Ada's father had given her. Black with embossed gilt symbols on the leather binding. It's a wonder to me that my hands still remember the weight and texture of it. The hands aren't as clever as the mind at retaining memories. You'll find the hands retain few memories. However, I still have one or two of Ada's memories hoarded in my hands, secreted in the tips of my fingers.'

I thought about this. And before I knew it my right hand was aflame with a memory of cupping Katie's crotch, of how snugly it fitted my palm, of how fluently and rewardingly she fed her pleasure into my fingertips.

'The first step in composing every spell was to hold hands and close our eyes. When I held Ada's hand I could feel things she left unsaid passing from her to me. To hold her hand was to welcome into my body the medium in which expectation exceeds circumstance. Which, if you think about it, is what magic is. I always found it easy to follow Ada in imagination and the further out she ventured the more exciting I found it to follow her. I feel she was the same with me, that she was by my side, holding my hand no matter how deep into my being my thoughts took me. So after long conversations with Ada who participated in my excitement with the exuberant empathy that characterised our bond I finally decided the moment had arrived to see what my mother looked like. She was as excited as I was to see my mother's face.

'Childhood for me might be best represented by the challenge of not making floorboards creak. I stole the photograph from Camille's jewellery box. It was a photograph of a painting.

Even though it was in black and white I could sense the colours were bold and vivacious. The woman in the painting was sitting in a chair, looking off into the distance. She looked sad. I decided this was because she had to give me away. No matter how hard I tried I couldn't make her catch my eye. She refused to look at me. I thought she was very beautiful but I always needed Ada's opinion before I could definitively give aesthetic value to any object. No one's opinions since have ever been more decisive to me than hers. So I was nervous before showing her the creased black and white photograph. It had snowed that day which was unusual in Paris. When we climbed up into our tree house the grass of the garden was still visible beneath the sprinkling of grains of ice. But then it began to fall more heavily. I have a memory of a bird alighting and leaving a few clawprints on the snow before it took off. I have a list over there on the wall of my favourite images. Birds and snow in the same frame is definitely a favourite. Perhaps because it's such an uncommon convergence. Like an annunciation.

'My small clouds of breath on the cold air were like the ghosts of the words I was too shy to say to Ada. I think I only said half of the things I wanted to say to her. That's probably true of everyone who loves. The unspoken declarations are like the genie in the bottle who never hears the magic word.

'Ada approved of my mother except she thought she was too young to be a mother.

'I usually carried that photograph around with me. It was like my identity card. One day I was walking with Ada along the quay, by the green book stalls, in sight of Notre-Dame. A group of boys was walking towards us. A boy who was in my class at school with his elder brother and three of his friends. They were the most glamorous peer group in the area as far as I was concerned. They organised the football games in which I longed to take part but from which I was always excluded. To be accepted by them was a recognition nearly all boys my age longed for. As if, instead of being just another pawn, you became one of the more powerful pieces on the chessboard. The elder brother whose name was Roland made a facetious remark about my relationship with Ada, using crude language. He referred to her as a dirty Jew. It was like he was trying to make me look as small as possible in front of Ada. It was unfair of him to bully me as he was three years older and much more powerfully built. I've always had a quick temper and my heartbeat was racing. I knew if I didn't stand up for Ada I would forever be ashamed of myself, shrunken, if not in her eyes, then in my own. So I made some crazy animal noises to connect me up to a store of madness within and shoved him in the chest. He quickly pinned my hands behind my back and told his brother to search me. His brother liked me; at least I had always believed he liked me. He pulled out the photograph of my mother and handed it to his brother. Roland looked at it for a moment then tore it in half. He put his face close to mine and tore it again and again and then threw the pieces into the Seine. I watched my mother, torn into small pieces, float off towards Notre-Dame.

'We decided to poison Roland. Ada's chemistry set came in handy here. We concocted in a glass vial a murky brown substance with a barely visible malevolent glitter. The idea was we would spread this potion inside a baguette with some ham and cheese and I would carry it in the hope our nemesis stole it and ate it. We were very pleased and excited with this idea. Until the day arrived to put it to the test. I imagined all kinds of outcomes. Primarily that he humiliated me again in front of Ada or that we killed him and I was sent to prison as a result. We took the poisoned baguette with us along the quay at a time we knew he would be returning home. But when he appeared he just ignored me and Ada. As if he had cancelled us both from his memory. Or perhaps got wind of our plan to poison him.

'We had a spell that would bring back a loved hour, enable us to relive it.

'We had a spell that would erase a bad memory.

'We had a spell that would make it snow.'

6 The Hunter and the Hunted

'Okay, let's see if I can do this chronologically. Paris during the war. One night I remember Paul was very upset. He was shouting at Camille and he looked like he had been crying. He rarely raised his voice. When someone you think you know well acts out of character it's like riding a bike that suddenly springs a puncture. At first, because children are egotistical, I thought I had done something to upset him. But Camille explained to me that he was upset because Russia had signed a pact with Germany. I thought this was a stupid reason to get upset. But it was the first sign something upsetting was happening in the world. In the following month some of the children at my school disappeared. We heard they had been taken to the country for their safety. Ada and I began to take more interest in the sky, as if at any moment bombs would start raining down on us. One night in our tree house Ada told me her parents were thinking of sending her away to relations in the country. For the first time I experienced a hint of what I stood to lose if Ada ever went away. I had a few other friends at school but they never remained my friends for long. They always discovered a better friend and then made a show of ignoring me. We devised a spell that would give us the power to cancel out anything her parents decided.

'Piles of sandbags began appearing in the city and the street lamps were dimmer at night. Traffic began dwindling. We watched the glass windows in Notre-Dame being taken down. Truth is, we were more excited than frightened.

'Then one day Camille sat me down opposite her. I could sense she was very agitated. At first I thought she was going to break up my friendship with Ada. It's always our worst fear that jumps out first when we're put into a state of alarm. I had assured myself no part of our sanctuary could be seen from Camille's bedroom window. I always suspected Camille of spying on me. In my head, she was like the secret police. Every secret I possessed had to be kept from her with unrelenting vigilance. Paul at this time was somewhere else. Maybe he was working outside Paris or maybe he was having an affair. In his absence Camille was much more needy around me. She was often trying to detain me from going outside. This meant I began avoiding eye contact with her. Otherwise she would begin talking to me and I would feel compelled to stay with her until she stopped. Sometimes I felt bad at how little interest I showed in what she said to me. That day she told me she had received a letter from my mother. She took it out of her bag and waved it at me. The paper was wafer thin and the sharply inked handwriting as exotic to me as hieroglyphics on ancient parchment. I could tell she didn't like this letter. That she wished it had never arrived. She told me my mother was coming to see me. But that I mustn't get too excited. I asked if my mother was coming to take me away. I was thinking of Ada. On the one hand there was nothing I wanted more than to know my mother and be with her; on the other, there was nothing I wanted less than to leave Ada. How helpless we are as children. Our hoard of treasure always at the mercy of adult whims. Camille told me she didn't know what my mother intended to do. That her letter wasn't clear on that point. She let slip that my mother sounded confused in the letter. I decided that this was because she still didn't know if she would like me or not. That she was coming to find this out. That seemed a reasonable explanation to me. Why would you want to live with someone you didn't like, even if they were your son? Therefore I had to make her like me. I didn't care much that other boys didn't seem to like me much. I had made Ada like me and this gave me all the confidence I needed. I decided I would convince my mother that she should stay with me in Paris. Camille would have to find somewhere else to live. I decided this was what I would tell Ada. That my mother was coming and if she found she liked me she was going to live with me in Paris. That way I knew Ada would be happy for me and would participate in my excitement – because this is what we did so well with each other. Together we taught each other how much exuberance our bodies and minds were capable of.

'When I screwed shut my eyes at night and concentrated I could still summon up the face of my mother in the photograph and I spoke to this face in my head but I still couldn't catch her eye nor elicit from her any answer to my questions.'

1 Dark Train

'On the day my mother was due to arrive Camille wouldn't let me wear the clothes I wanted to wear. My play clothes with their stains and rips and friendly soft touch against my skin. Instead I had to wear a blue beret I hated, trousers that scratched my legs and a sleeveless pullover that was too tight under the arms. My revenge was to refuse her hand when we went to the Gare de Lyon. I sometimes made a game of pretending Camille was a witch and thus it was imperative that I never allowed her to touch me. I never liked being touched by her. And she knew this, which makes me feel bad now. I tried to picture what kind of hat my mother would wear to meet me. I remember standing on the ramp outside the station looking down at all the wet coloured lights on the pavement. Those bright glistening reds, greens and blues were like the colours my new life with my mother would be dipped in. When the train arrived I couldn't concentrate on any of the women walking towards me through the swirl of steam down the platform. My eyes were jumping about like firecrackers. Then the platform was empty. I refused to believe she wasn't on the train. I dug in my heels and demanded we wait for the next train. Camille told me there wasn't another train.

I decided my mother had decided that she didn't like me enough to come. I endowed her with supernatural powers. She didn't have to meet me to establish that she didn't like me enough. My mother froze into a queen made of ice for me that day. Every time I thought about her it was like a cold draught made my body shiver and I had to hug warmth back into my body.

'I crept out of our apartment that night. To get into Ada's garden there was a secret opening in a hedge which was difficult to find in the dark. But I was angry with life and I enjoyed hurting my body, the pricking of needles on my palms, the scratching of thorns on my cheeks, the stones chaffing my knees. Wispy things I couldn't see brushed my face, like the touch of a ghost. The tree, embossed on the dark and swollen to immense proportions by its shadow, frightened me. It was the first time it hadn't appeared to me as my friend. My heart was thumping when I climbed up the ladder. I expected Ada to know I was there. But she didn't come. I stayed there for a long time, aware of movements in the shadows. Eventually, when my eyes had grown accustomed to the darkness, a fox entered the garden. It was like a magical creature underneath the moon. I watched it brush itself against the leaves of bushes. I watched it squat down and urinate. She was leaving her scent. I decided I would copy her. That I too would leave my scent. She ran off when she saw me. I stood on the top rung of the ladder and pissed down on the grass. This made me laugh out loud. I think that was the first time I discovered there was a vein of frightening madness in me. I came to think of this part of myself as the stairway in a bombed out building that only leads up into the sky.

'We had a spell that would make us invisible.

'We had a spell that made her become a boy and made me become a girl.

'We had a spell that enabled us to speak any language we wished.'

8 Damage

'You know what happened next. The Nazis invaded Poland; France declared war. You might think that when you hear news like that you realise how insignificant most other news is. But I was much more frightened by the news I heard that a snake had been found on the balcony of one of our neighbours. I still now check for snakes whenever I go out onto a balcony.

'However, war was declared and everyone began to look like they had seen a ghost. There was more interest in people's eyes. The radio played nothing but military music. You often saw people carrying their belongings on their backs or pushing them about on carts. Everyone wanted to be somewhere else. Except Ada and me. I saw off Paul with Camille at the Gare de l'Est. He was going off to be a soldier. He looked shrunken, like an abandoned child, when he climbed aboard the train. He was going to Nancy and from there to the Maginot line. I liked Paris better without so many men. It seemed kinder to the imagination and to favourite feelings. The scent of the flowers seemed more prominent. Lots of people I was used to seeing every day vanished. They left secret openings that hadn't been there before. Again Ada's parents discussed moving to the country. Again we created a spell to ensure this wouldn't happen. More likely though it was Ada's father's indecisiveness which ensured Ada remained my playmate. I think he had worked so hard to get where he was and become respected that he couldn't face the thought of starting all over from scratch. He was stuck in his ways. A fatal condition for any Jew in a Nazi occupied country.

'Soon the air raid alarm kept going off. I enjoyed this because it usually happened in the middle of the night and Camille would hurry me down into the basement of Ada's building. No lights were allowed and the stars always seemed far more numerous and brighter and closer. Sounds were more vivid too. You could hear the sigh of the river's tide as if it was part of your own breathing. What was most exciting was that I got to see Ada at times when before she had been off-limits. I got to see her in her nightclothes with the smell and sheen of sleep on her. And because it was so crowded we always sat squashed together on a bench, our hips and thighs pressed into each other. For the first time I discovered how much excitement there was in the intimate contact of her body. Our relationship changed down in that cellar. It was like the fumes of that cramped underworld place led my thoughts down into darker parts of my own being.

'I remember everyone was frightened of the Nazis dropping poisonous gas on Paris. There was a brochure in our apartment giving instructions as to what to do if a gas attack arrived. And people were angry because there weren't enough gas masks to go round. There was one woman in the shelter who always wore her mask. There were often arguments. No pets were allowed but an old woman always brought her cat. Ada and I liked this woman and we liked her cat too. But other people tried to force her to leave the cat outside. Soon she stopped coming to the shelter. I became aware down in that shelter that some people didn't like Ada's parents. This was especially true of the concierge of their apartment, a prying busybody of a woman who was always rolling her eyes and making disdainful noises with her tongue. I found out why one night when Ada and her parents didn't come down to the shelter and the concierge asked with a sneer where the Jews were tonight and another woman pulled a disgusted face. Both of these women became archenemies of mine. I was too shy to make it plain how much I disliked them but they were high up on my list of hoped for casualties if a bomb did fall. There was also a man I disliked because he was always trying to attract Ada's attention. It was like he believed he shared a running joke with Ada and he only had to look at her to start the joke up again. I never knew what this joke was. I don't think Ada did either. Usually I liked anyone who liked Ada but I didn't like him. If I had to choose ten casualties of a bomb, a pastime I enjoyed in the shelter when Ada wasn't there, he was on my list too. He was the only one on my list Ada thought shouldn't be included and the fact that he was became the cause of a disagreement between us which made me dislike him even more. But even though alarms often sent us down to the shelter nothing actually happened. There was no more sign of a war now than there had been the year before. It was like some mad game the adults had decided to play. To pretend there was a war when there was no sign whatsoever of this being the case. But more familiar people began disappearing – the artist who sat on a stool painting on the bridge, the man in the yellow and blue barge that was always on the river when I came home from school. And some shops were boarded up. That too was like a mad game. As if there were a contest to see who would be the last person not to leave Paris.

'Without so much traffic the avenues seemed wider, infinite with distance which was both exciting and frightening. At times it was so quiet you felt you could almost hear the future arriving.

'But then of course the Nazis finally turned up, in startling technicolour. We weren't allowed to see them arrive. Everybody was forbidden to leave their homes for forty-eight hours. I would have been happy if this law continued forever because it meant Ada and I had more time in our tree house. When we were allowed out again there were some Nazis around Notre-Dame. Mostly handsome young men in elegant uniforms trying to contain their excitement. They were glamorous figures to begin with. What little boy isn't attracted to uniforms and guns? Before Ada arrived lead soldiers and model aeroplanes had been my favourite toys. Ada though hated the soldiers. She had been forbidden by her father to even look at them. It was the first sign of an emotional buffer between us. She recognised them for what they were. But I was fascinated by people from foreign lands. They had an air of confidence, security and impunity which set them apart from the people I was used to seeing. I saw them as offering clues as to what my mother was like. I wondered if any of them knew my mother. To my unformed mind this didn't seem a far-fetched possibility.

'It was less the soldiers and more the enormous Nazi flags draped over buildings which brought home how altered reality was. The most immediate effect of that red and white flag with the black swastika was one of unfriendliness. It made the familiar look unreal. Like waking up into a dream. It seemed to steal one's memories. Steal the substance from everything it presided over. The sight of it always made me feel a bit dizzy as if I was filled with hot air.

9 The Sailor and the Animals

'Ada's apartment had a distinctive pervasive smell. It created a kind of hush in the air that seemed to tunnel back into the past. Memory was a richer presence in her home than mine. I decided this fascinating smell was what made them Jewish. Because I couldn't detect any other differences between Ada's parents and Paul and Camille. After Roland called Ada a dirty Jew we talked about her being Jewish a few times. I learned she went to a synagogue and not a church. And there were rituals at the kitchen table which Paul and Camille didn't perform. The only ritual at our table was to finish eating as quickly as possible so we no longer suffered the discomfort of having to keep up conversation. One time Ada and I discussed what would happen if the whole world suddenly stopped praying.'

'What do you think would happen?'

'I suspect the world would soon become either a better or a worse place,' he said and winked at me. 'One day, before the Jews were made to wear the yellow star, I went to the zoo with Ada and her parents and a German sailor lifted me up and pretended he was going to throw me into the lion pit. I caught the eye of one lioness in particular. I watched her slowly lick her lips with her huge tongue. Then she yawned and showed me all her teeth. When he put me down he asked me if I was a Jew. Ada was standing next to me. He told me I was lucky I wasn't a Jew and made a throat slitting gesture and tried to make me laugh by pulling the face of a hanged man with crossed eyes and his tongue lolling out. 'What an idiot,' I said to Ada when he was out of hearing range, trying to bridge a gap that had suddenly materialised between our solitudes. But Ada didn't smile or answer and for the rest of the day I felt like I had a sharp stone in my shoe.

10 Dreams Never End

'The first time we played our naughty game Ada was wearing the yellow star on her left breast. I don't now remember how this game was initiated. The moment of extreme daring when it must have been suggested by one or the other of us. I can't quite believe that daring came from me but then neither can I quite believe it came from Ada. I have to think of it as a spontaneous reaction of our alchemy. I had discovered it was thrilling to be touched by Ada on my bare skin. She seemed to enjoy these games too but I have a horror now that maybe I was coercing her into doing something which troubled her when she was alone in her bed at night. That she was going out of her way to please me because the rest of the world had made her feel so lonely and unwanted. Touch – it's such a natural human impulse but how complex and dark are the labyrinths of emotion it can lead us into. The yellow star subtly shifted the balance of power in our relationship. It made her more alone. And it made me more protective of her which was to admit a new vulnerability in her. We ceased to be quite equals. You know how in every relationship there's the lover and the beloved? Before there had been no sense of a distinction between us. Now I became like the beloved, called upon to provide reassurance. The primary condition of the beloved is to take. But the soul likes to give better than it likes to take. Of course most of all it likes to share.

'Sometimes I could see through her thin cotton dress. It makes me uncomfortable now to think of that. I'm an old man marvelling at the naked grace of an eleven year old girl. Except of course we're never quite so categorically prisoners of the count of time as appearances would suggest.

'I remember the day after Ada's father lost his job. I can't remember what he did. Something to do with selling insurance maybe. Which is so perversely ironic I fear I might have made it up. He would sit in a room shadowy with dark furniture, dusty rugs, curtains and brocades. There were old prints on the walls that spoke of secret histories. Ada's apartment was much more lovingly maintained than Camille's. There was no flaking whitewash on the walls, no rust on the metalwork, no ingrained stains on the enamels. That day he looked like someone whose powers and beliefs had all failed him. So glum that Ada suggested we cheer him up. We did this by dressing up in her mother and father's clothes. I was dressed as Ada's mother and wore a long violet dress which draped over the floor around me like a bridal dress. Ada made me up in the mirror. She painted my lips and eyes and dusted powder over my cheeks. She dressed up in a black suit of her father's and heavy shoes which were much too big for her and she slid about in like an ice skater. I drew a black moustache above her top lip. When we went downstairs I was carrying a briefcase and she wore a feathered hat and carried a green handbag. We entered the room arm in arm. Her father smiled briefly when he saw us but then he began crying. This wasn't at all the effect we had hoped to create.

'I also remember Ada's father told her she had to wear the star with pride. I imagined it like being forced to wear the dunce cap at school. I think that's how Ada saw it too. Camille had advised me not to go out in the streets with Ada and her parents now that the yellow star drew attention to them as outcasts. She said it was in my own best interests. More than ever I pretended she was a witch. One time, a French policeman stopped us and asked why I wasn't wearing a yellow star. I was struck by how kind and respectful Ada's father was to this hateful little man bloated with his own authority. How obsequious. I could sense Ada was a little ashamed of her father at that moment. It was the only time I ever saw her not enjoy the emotions her father inspired in her. He explained that I was a friend of Ada's and not a Jew. The policeman looked down at me with scorn. He went straight to the top of the list of the people I wanted a bomb to fall on. British bombs at this time occasionally fell on Paris.

'Whenever I went outside with Ada while she was wearing the yellow star on her chest I noticed how often people smiled upon seeing it. And it was difficult to work out if they were smiling in sympathy or scorn. I knew from experience how sensitive children are to anything that makes them stand out. Camille had knitted me a pullover with a white flower over my heart. Everyone at school laughed at me for wearing this pullover.

'I wasn't brave or forthright in my feeling of support in those days. I'd like to say that whenever Ada wore the yellow star I wanted to rip it off and throw it in the gutter. Perhaps that was true. I did hate it because of how much distress and humiliation I could tell it caused her. But now and again I had doubts. Kids who had never shown the slightest interest in heritage began singling out Jewish kids for their insults. It was like a new trend and you know how quickly and unanimously trends take hold of kids. Probably the inspiration for this hostility came from their parents. I still wanted to be with Ada as much as ever but I became perhaps more intent on hiding our relationship from the world. I enjoyed her company much more in our tree house than in the outside world. In the outside world I didn't like all the attention we attracted together. It felt like the whole world was trying to break up our friendship. Maybe Ada sensed this withdrawal on my part and it was a desire to keep me close that led to the naughty games. Even talking about those times now, all these years later, I want to grind my own head into the dirt.

'I remember half the things in our apartment stopped working. The heating and hot water for example. We had a wood fire in the living room but no wood. Ada told me her father had an argument with a woman who wanted to chop off branches of our tree, even burn the wood with which he had built our house. We gave this woman the evil eye at every opportunity. But it was the first indication the days of our tree house were numbered. Camille's fingers were all swollen up and ugly. Chilblains. She began crying a lot. I could hear her when I was in bed. There was never enough to eat. Never anything nice to eat.'

11 Seeing Out the Angel

'We're now coming towards the day in July 1942 when Roland's brother invited me to play football with Roland's gang. One of the boys who usually played had been taken to the Free Zone by his parents. They were a player short. There was now an opening for me. I realised how important it was to me to be accepted by this group of boys. That Ada wasn't enough. I was weary of being an outcast. I wanted to belong. I didn't tell Ada. It was the first time I had ever withheld an exciting piece of news from her. I had to defend myself in my head from an accusation I was betraying her. Some of these boys, after all, were Jew haters and enjoyed hurting Ada.

'I was scared of not acquitting myself well when I arrived in the small park. That's all I remember about that game of football. I remember the aftermath though. We all walked towards the river together. The boys included me in their boyish high spirits and camaraderie. Then I saw Ada and her parents walking towards us, each wearing the gaudy yellow star. Roland saw them too and put his arm around my shoulder. He was forbidding me to greet Ada. It was as plain to me as if he spoke the words aloud. I could immediately sense she was horrified that I was in the company of these bully boys and a defiant and defensive impulse took me over. I pretended not to notice her. I could sense the pain this snub of mine caused her father. He appeared more hurt than Ada herself. I looked back over my shoulder after we had crossed paths. The Orpheus moment. I felt awful when I arrived home. Sick to my stomach. I needed to conform, to belong. Ada never gave me that. The tree house had an atmosphere of being far removed from the streets, immune to all the forces of the everyday world. It was like a raft far out at sea.

'I prepared a speech of apology to Ada. In my imagination she eventually smiled and forgave me. I was confident I could bring about this outcome when I climbed up into the tree house. But I was nervous of her father. Every time I remembered the hurt I had caused him I felt sick. However neither Ada nor her father appeared. And our book of spells was missing. It was a law that no one was allowed to ever remove the book from the tree house.

'I didn't then know I had seen Ada for the last time. There was no forewarning. That night the Vel' d'Hiv roundup took place and Ada and her parents were among those taken to the velodrome and from there, eventually, to Auschwitz.'

My grandfather slapped his right cheek with his right hand, then he slapped his left cheek with his left hand. His black-framed glasses slid down his nose at an askew angle. He carried on slapping himself until I told him to stop.

12 To Heal

I understood his need to be accepted by the other boys and I tried to tell him so by recounting to him one of my own memories that he had participated in. It was the first time I saw my name on the team sheet for my school's next football match. I was in the year below most of the boys in the team so it was a prestigious achievement on my part. My grandfather was the only member of my family who understood this. And he came to watch.

'Like you I have little memory of that game except, now, all of a sudden, I remember the shin pads I was wearing and the suspicion that I barely touched the ball. Do you remember watching?'

'Your first touch was a misplaced pass and with your second you dithered and were tackled. A crunching tackle that left you splayed in the mud. I don't think you were very keen to get the ball after that. You had the thinnest legs of any boy on the field. I remember fearing for your safety. I remember the pitch was flanked by creosoted wooden fences and behind those fences were the small gardens of identical houses. And that the pitch sloped and was a mud bath. When the game finished none of your teammates talked to you. You walked off the pitch alone. I knew you weren't very pleased with your performance because you refused to catch my eye. For me personally the experience was an agony of helplessness. It was like praying and knowing the thing you prayed for was never going to happen.'

'Was I that bad?'

'You weren't so much bad as opposed to the spirit of the game. You didn't want the ball.'

'I'm still like that. I still don't want the ball,' I said.

My grandfather struggled to his feet and mimed a throw-in at me. I took the imaginary ball on my chest and sidefooted it back to him.

'You were very lucky to get born,' he said, after settling himself back into his chair. 'That is, of course, if you like your life. If you don't, then you were no less *un*lucky to get born. Because your grandmother and I only did the deed one time. I don't have much imagination. I have to do things before I know whether or not I want to do them. Like I had to play football with Roland and his gang before I found out that wasn't what I wanted at all. So I had to have sex with your grandmother before I knew that wasn't something I would be able to continue doing. I felt like I was betraying Ada all over again. I thought the least I could do for betraying her that afternoon was to do penitence by not replacing her. Also, I wasn't wholly won over by the adult version of orgasm. For starters, it's unreliable; it changes one's mood, like dreams. It's like a pyrotechnic eviction from the embrace of all one's comforting yearnings and their occult energies. Of course it may be that what happened to Ada is responsible for my uneasy relationship with orgasm.'

'Do I really want to hear this?' I said, squeezing together my hands.

'Oh stop pretending you're a prude. What are you, a dedicated *Daily Mail* reader?' This time he performed a seated dance, his hands tracing serpent undulations on the air. I noticed his head always inclined towards his right shoulder. It made him look like he humorously doubted everything he said. I realised my head too slanted towards my right shoulder.

'Your grandmother rather bullied me into marrying her. She wore down my resistance. I never understood why she wanted to marry me so much. Later on in her life she would make a habit of taking in dogs from animal rescue centres. I believe she now has seven. I suppose I was the first. I ended up thinking if she wants to marry me so much isn't it mean-spirited to refuse to grant her wish? I'm far too passive by nature. Also, her parents agreed to pay for the honeymoon which I demanded should be in Venice. This gave me the opportunity to look for my mother. I was convinced that only by knowing who my mother was might help me escape the curse of who I had become. Sometimes life can create a new set of circumstances for you that completely override the old set. Because that afternoon on the quay had pushed me through a door into a place I never should have entered and there was no way for me to get back to where I had lived before. I felt as though the tape on which my life was recorded had snapped. The two shredded ends were whirling around on different spools, forever now separated. But no story should end in shame. We have to believe in the possibility of atonement if we're going to carry on living. So I got married.

'Perhaps it might seem to you that I'm giving myself airs by imposing my petty guilt on the magnitude of the tragedy that befell Ada. But you need to understand Ada is my faith, not my despair. And faith is something that should always be passed on from generation to generation. This is why I'm telling you my story. Not to garner sympathy or invite judgement. I hope you will eventually understand this.'

'I'll do my best,' I said.

'After I lost the tree house I faced a reality bereft of magic. I've never lost my belief in magic; it's just that I became incapable of performing it anymore. It wasn't only Ada who vanished that night. It was me too. I vanished. And I've been trying to find myself ever since.'

13 All My Colours

'I expect you're wondering about the naughty games. Eventually everything brought up into the tree house had to first go through a ritual. The ritual was that I would blindfold Ada. I would then hide the new treasure somewhere on my person and she would have to find it before an hourglass ran out. To begin with the exploration of her hands was chaste. But we soon both grew impatient with this charade of innocence. As young as we were we both knew where the heartbeat of all my hot pleasure was located. Thus I began to know the pleasure of her inquisitive hands rooting about in my trouser pockets, probing up the insides of my legs, sliding over the skin below my ribcage. For a while there was a reciprocated shyness about her touching me there. I might hide the treasure just beneath the top button of my trousers but never lower down. I don't know why the roles were never reversed. I never wanted to touch her in the places she differed from me. I suspect because she didn't want me to touch her in those places and I picked this up.

'Sometimes I think Ada had an inkling somewhere in her body or her mind of what was going to happen to her, that she would never make it into adulthood and her deeply protective housekeeping of the tree house and the erotic games we played there were her only chance of experiencing herself as a wife. Had she lived I'm certain we would have married. You might think it just a childish fancy of mine but it's one of the very few things I've remained certain about during the course of my life. And my life has borne out that she was the only wife for me. I could tell she was a female for all the times of my life. It was the way we could light each other up. The way we could heighten each other's attention. Unlike poor Prufrock we could hear the mermaids singing to each other when we were together.

'Anyway, I was discovering a new and illicit source of pleasure in my body. I began to take little interest in all the other things we did and said together. The book of spells became little more an excuse to get her to put her hands on my body. The book of spells had done its work. I knew now the nature of its magic. I arranged to meet Ada in the tree house after dark. I went out into the night in my pyjamas. I plucked up the courage to hide a strand of red thread deep down in my underpants. The sand ran down more than once but I pretended it hadn't. I knew she had found the thread but was pretending not to have. Her fingers kept sliding over my tiny erection. I sensed she was as curious as I was about what would happen. At that age there's nothing as riotous as ejaculation. The booster charger isn't functioning yet. More an escalating tingling which culminates in a glowing seep of stickiness. I was embarrassed by the sticky wetness. It was the only part of the rite I didn't enjoy. I was embarrassed until, another time, Ada brought it out into the open by suggesting without any hint of disdain that we use my hot sticky stuff for a spell. This time there was no pretence of finding anything hidden in my underpants. She simply set out to extract some seed from my burning body. I'll never forget the reverential way she collected the sample on her fingertip. It was the most trusting and intimate exchange yet between us. My body sharing its secret with her. A starburst of amazement holding us in its electrifying grip. I can't remember what spell Ada's fingerprint of my glistening filament in the black book came to signify. Perhaps a spell that could change us into an animal of our choosing.

'To escape my last memory of Ada I tried to replace it with the recollection of our last afternoon in the tree house. I couldn't believe there had been no forewarning of our separation. Couldn't believe I had forgotten the last words she ever said to me, the last look she gave me. I knew we hadn't played our naughty game that day. She hadn't wanted to. I wondered if she thought I ignored her because I was annoyed by her refusal to pleasure me. There are few worst feelings than being denied the relief of explaining away a fatal misunderstanding to a loved one. It makes you hate the dreary linear nature of time. If there's a God why didn't He come up with a more creative way for us to experience time? Why, for example, can't we physically go back in time at least once in our lives instead of this feeble scrabbling back in imagination and memory?'

14 The Thin Air

'I now felt a deep sulking loathing for the Nazi soldiers. One day a uniformed member of the Third Reich was kind to me. He tried to talk to me in broken French, he kept smiling at me, desperate for me to smile back at him. I thought the Germans were stupid because not many of them could speak French. He gave me some chocolate. I felt grubby for showing him some gratitude. When he turned his back I took out my fountain pen and flicked a trail of ink spots down the back of his crisp grey-green uniform. I threw the chocolate away even though I hadn't eaten anything sweet for months. That didn't make me feel any better though. I didn't know any more what was right and what was wrong.

'Sometimes at night the only sound was the syncopated footfalls of a Nazi patrol stiffly marching past in their nailed boots. It was like the noise of a pitiless machine. The sound of those unseen boots created an abyss in the atmosphere that you felt yourself falling into. You can't imagine how sinister it seemed that they marched in step like that when there was no one around to see them. They didn't seem like human beings, more like programmed automatons.

'But it wasn't the Nazis who took Ada away. I found out

later that it was three French policeman who had arrested Ada and her parents. I wanted to know who these men were. I wanted to make known to them how much I wished them dead. It still seems surreal to me that every death was bureaucratically detailed and plotted. That Ada was on a file in an office. That there were officials with combed hair and polished shoes who transferred her details from one chit of paper to another. The only person I knew who had seen the arresting policemen was the concierge. She tried to make out to me she was sorry that Ada had been arrested but I could tell she thought Ada deserved it. There was a policeman who lived further down our street and I asked if he had been one of the men. He wasn't but that didn't stop me hating him and his ticket collector hat and vainglory cape. Several times I had seen him salute when German soldiers walked past him. The next time I saw him I saluted him. Except he thought I was in earnest and smiled at me good naturedly. He didn't get it that I was telling him to drop dead. The Nazis were good at creating hatred. And when you hate you feel a need to triumph. That triumph Hitler knew for a while but it was always denied to me.

'Mostly in life we like to think of ourselves as autonomous, intrepid buccaneers beating down obstacles, but there are moments when it's expedient to see ourselves as puppets. Most people were probably happy to think of themselves as puppets during the Nazi occupation. To shirk all responsibility. To idle in a convenient state of servitude. We all fashion ourselves to the false world in which we live and in so doing become false ourselves. I saw this all the time during the occupation. How people could convince themselves that locking up and deporting Jews, including children, was a rational consequence of events. How the same people who shrugged off news of executions and deportations were beside themselves with rage when someone tried to jump a queue. I understand now that many of those policeman were driven by an impulse not unlike mine with Roland and his gang. It takes more courage than most people have not to submit to the pressure to conform. We copy our neighbour much more than we are willing to admit. It's difficult to cleave to what little independence of thought we all possess in the face of hostility. I often wonder about those three policeman now. Are they still alive? And if so how do they feel about what they did? Now they know what happened to the people they arrested do the faces of those people haunt them? Do they still remember the child they arrested? Is there another man out there who is tormented every day of his life for betraying Ada? I like to think we all have our own inner tribunal. And it's this tribunal that always has the last word.

'A few weeks later some men arrived in a truck to take away things in Ada's house. I stood on the pavement opposite and watched. I saw them carry out the living room rugs, the bed linen, crockery and the old prints that hung on the walls. I was looking for our book of spells but if they took it I didn't see it. When they left I asked the concierge if I could go into Ada's apartment. She wouldn't let me. She told me there was a seal on the door. Whenever I got the chance I gave her the evil eye and it pleased me to see she was discomforted by my obvious hostility towards her.

'I couldn't stand the sight of Roland and ignored him. I no longer harboured any aspirations to play football with his gang. I learned later that Roland's mother had died when he was young and his drunken Jew-hating father beat him. Some people, call them largely ignorant unimaginative people, feel a need to inflict their own emotional pain on others in the form of physical pain. The war was created by such people.

'I spent hours in queues with Camille. We queued for things that were no longer there when we reached the counter. An eloquent metaphor for the life of a demoralised individual. I remember she wore a grey and pink shawl and knitted heavy black stockings that looked like boots. I had no new toys, no new comics, no new clothes. I had to make do with what I already had, as did everyone. This was another obstacle to moving forward. At the lycée opposite the Luxembourg Gardens I now attended I was asked where my Jew girlfriend was and there would be sniggers. I got into lots of fights. I threw myself at anyone who took Ada's name in vain. I enjoyed the pain of being beaten. I enjoyed the marks on my face. They were like something I could offer Ada as recompense. But eventually my fighting skills improved and boys were less keen to goad me. I was left alone. I'm not saying I didn't have friends or no longer laughed during that period but these were trivial asides and have no part to play in my story. There are entire years in my life like that. I think Camille began to despair of me and that's why, one evening, she decided to tell me a few things about my mother. Camille had studied for a year in Venice and lived with my mother's family. I can't have been very interested because I don't remember now anything she said. I didn't like my mother anymore. I kept thinking that if she had come to Paris that day and taken me away I wouldn't have betrayed Ada. Ada would still be dead but at least I would be able to remember her without hating myself. Camille promised me we would go to Italy when the war ended and find her. I was fifteen when the war ended. We didn't go to Italy.

'I had neglected the tree house after Ada left. It made me feel alone and weightless to sit up there without her. When I returned after the war, channelling all my energy into willing Ada to be sitting up there, webs clung to my face and hair and one of the buckled floorboards sprang up like a pushed piano key. I remember watching a bird down on the grass and because it seemed to know I was there even if it didn't look at me I thought for a moment that maybe Ada had come back as a bird. Birds make you feel that sometimes about the dead.

'But I felt betrayed by our tree house. It was as if it had forgotten Ada.

'Then one day at school there were excited rumours. News of the gas chambers had arrived. Even though I was now fifteen I found it difficult to form a conceivable picture of what I was being told.

'Paul never came home. He died in Germany of exhaustion or typhus. Camille wrote to my mother but received no answer. I no longer pretended Camille was a witch.

'We heard from the concierge that Ada and her parents had been gassed. A relative of the family who had eluded the Nazis paid a visit to the apartment. The concierge put on a show of being outraged by the news. I found out the details piece by piece. Eventually I learned the date. The third of September, 1942. I drove myself half mad trying to recall how I had spent that day. I wrote Ada lots and lots of letters in those days. But always in my head. I never put a single word to paper. So I had no record of that day. I made a list of all the things I knew I had done, because I did them every day. That's probably when my need of lists was born. Maybe while Ada was being gassed I was watering the tray of leeks Camille had planted in a box in the living room. Maybe I was looking at my face in the bathroom mirror while brushing my teeth. I hoped it had been one of the days I was bloodied and bruised in the school playground. That I hadn't been happy at any time that day.

'I also found out Ada hadn't arrived at Auschwitz with her mother and father. Her parents were murdered a month earlier. She had been herded off to another camp in France with all the other children. She arrived at Auschwitz, an eleven year old girl, without her mother or father.

'When we're seized by grief what we most want is to stand out in the rain. Stand out in the rain refusing all shelter. At every opportunity I stand out in the rain. I find it always helps.'

15 Love Will Tear Us Apart

My grandfather gave me a sad smile. I nodded my head in sympathy. At times of heightened emotional pain like this perhaps only a quote from the Bible or Shakespeare can meet the need for consolatory eloquence and unfortunately I had no quotes from either memorised, appropriate or otherwise. I had though been thinking about love.

Love for nearly everyone I've known has been essentially expedient. A sensible investment. Obsessive romantic love, which is what my grandfather seemed to be in the prey of, is to make one person the sole custodian of your self-esteem. To me there's a propensity to self-harm in such an investment. I was under no illusion that Katie, by taking me back, could restore to me my mental health. I sometimes wondered how generous, how understanding she might have been had I told her the truth. Over time I knew she would have become impatient with the long list of things I was no longer able to do. That was only natural.

Though I no longer had Katie, in many ways I was stuck with her, just as my grandfather was stuck with Ada. I could no more replace Katie than he could replace Ada. The state I was in no one else was going to date me. I was someone who relentlessly came up with elaborate excuses for not doing things everyone else loved doing. Perhaps, without my affliction, I would have replaced her by now. I can't say sex between us was better than what I had known before with other girls. On that score she would be replaceable. The intimacy we shared too could probably be replicated with time. I'd still miss her though. Most of all I'd miss watching her dance. That after all was a gift she had that wasn't easily replaceable. And it saddened me that I missed the flowering of her gift. Because obviously the stuff she does with Pina Bausch is a lot more accomplished than anything I saw her do. So I wasn't sure I bought into my grandfather's conviction of one life, one love. There was a lot of pathology in his feeling for Ada, something, as I said, wilfully self-harming, like a razor with which he cut himself. At the same time his pain made him beguiling, made him loveable. There was something noble and heartwarming about his fidelity. You could always see the child in his eyes.

I did though wonder if my grandfather hadn't used Ada as an excuse not to exert himself in life. Just as I wondered if my discomfort in the social world wasn't an elaborate excuse brewed up by my mind for retreating to my room which is where I was most happy as a child.

16 Seen and Not Seen

'What do you remember about me?' I asked him. I'm not sure I was particularly interested in what he remembered about me; it was more that I was growing uncomfortable with all his highly charged emotion as if before long he might break down and I might be called upon to offer solace in the form of a hug. My entire family has an almost pathological aversion to resorting to physical contact with each other which has perhaps reached its zenith in me.

'This would be a good subject for one of my memory lists,' he said. 'I remember you had an Action Man but you never seemed convinced by him. There wasn't much of a connection between you and him. Though I recall you liked the parachute he had. You became interested in heights. You climbed as high as you could so as to drop him. His parachute though didn't slow his descent at all. Perhaps that was the moment you ceased to believe in magic and first crossed the threshold between the expectations of a child and those of an adult. I remember you liked to watch *Top Cat*, *Bewitched* and *Dr Who*. And I remember that scene in the credits of *The Flintstones* when Fred is dumped down outside his house and locked out disturbed you. Were you frightened of being locked out of your home? Or was that how you felt all the time? I suspected it might be the latter. Your mother was uncomfortable in her role as mother. I used to wonder if that was my fault. I remember you were always down on your knees playing Subbuteo in your room. You commentated aloud on all the matches you played. And you wrote down the scores, goalscorers and league tables in blue exercise books. I remember often I didn't feel much older than you were. And I felt a fake every time I tried to play the adult and mentor.

'One memory I have of you as a child is watching you burying something in the garden at the house in St Mary's Bay. Do you remember that house?'

'We went there on holiday every year for a while. It had a painted glass window of red roses. It darkened the light and tinted it red and green in the living room. And we played Old Maid at the table in the evenings because there was no television.'

'I don't remember that. But I remember watching you through the window one afternoon. Your father's red MG was parked on the gravel. I never understood why such a self-effacing man had such an ostentatious car. That car was like a Freudian slip. Anyway, you were burying something. Over in the corner of the garden where a tree grew on a slope. That night your mother asked if anyone had seen her favourite lipstick. I kept quiet but I knew now what you had been so surreptitiously burying.'

He grinned at me.

'I think you're making this up,' I said. 'I don't remember that. Why would I bury mum's lipstick?'

'Perhaps it embarrassed you?'

'Embarrassed me in front of who?'

'There was a girl on the beach you liked that year.'

'I don't remember that either. I think you're trying to force on me memories that don't belong to me,' I said.

'Just because you don't remember something doesn't mean it didn't happen.'

I was struck by the mischief in his eyes. His face seemed to be telling me more than his words. For a moment I harboured the suspicion that my grandfather's entire narrative was a fiction, like this memory of me I was sure he had invented. That maybe his narrative was some kind of elaborate justification for his failures as a husband and a father. Because, despite all his charm, I knew he had caused several people a good deal of pain, not least of all, my mother. Perhaps there had never been any Ada.

'How come you don't have a photograph of Ada?'

'Who says I don't?'

'Do you? I'd like to see it.'

'I don't. Children don't need photographs,' he said.

'You needed the photograph of your mother,' I countered.

'I had no memory of ever seeing my mother. I saw Ada every day. Have you got photos of your early childhood friends?'

I had to admit I didn't. I spent a few moments trying to remember who my early childhood friends were, what they looked like, what they meant to me. I was struck by how irrelevant they all seemed now.

17 Nostalgia

My grandfather lived with my parents when I was growing up. I don't think my father approved of this but his will was weaker than that of my mother. He used to play football with me in the garden. I remember the sound the studs of my football boots made on the patio paving stones. It was a good feeling as a child to hear one's passage make such a far-reaching din.

One evening he took me to see Chelsea play at Stamford Bridge. I remember the closer you got to the ground the more contagious became the excited air of expectation. It was a big part of everyone's mood, pervasive like a smell. The kind of thing you ought to feel when going to church. We moved through the heat and stink of the hot dog stalls outside the ground. Everyone was wearing blue and white scarves, even the old men. Age mattered less here. It was probably the first time I had felt part of a community. Not spinning around in an orbit of my own.

The moment I first caught sight of the pitch washed in floodlights was like standing on tiptoes and peeping at a world I was forbidden to enter. Never had I seen colours ache with such pristine beauty. The tiny players in their royal blue kits, the green grass and its chalked white lines looked like some magical kingdom beneath the liquid snow of the floodlights. I was enraptured but I contained my joy. Later I became engrossed in the abuse and hatred focused on the away supporters at the other end of the ground. This hatred I noticed was a bond between the males. It enabled them to touch and hug each other, to swear and shout and laugh, to sometimes get angry which they enjoyed. Half way during the game my grandfather got up from his seat and without any explanation made for the exit. I thought he might have gone off to buy me a hotdog or a drink. He liked giving me treats. Every Thursday he brought me home a copy of *The Beano*, a bag of sweets and an ice cream. He called it Chocolate Thursday. Before long I realised he wasn't coming back. I spent the rest of the game trying to map my way home in my mind. This was the first time I can recall being panicked in the midst of people.

I did find my way home and was feeling very proud of myself but my father was furious as if it was my fault that my grandfather had abandoned me. There was an angry exchange between my parents. I felt much closer to my grandfather than to either of my parents. I did my best to defend him. My parents made it clear my opinion was worthless. In the middle of the night I was woken by the breaking of glass. My grandfather came home drunk and broke a bottle of wine in the kitchen. It wasn't long after this night that he vanished from my life for years on end. Within months I became a rebel. I picked fights with both my parents at every opportunity. I don't remember ever admitting to myself that I missed my grandfather.

'What happened when you had your breakdowns?' I asked. My curiosity was in the nature of research. I thought it only a matter of time before I ended up in some psychiatric ward. It was the vista I most often saw when I looked into the future.

'I don't want to talk about those times,' he said.

18 A History of Holes

'Okay. What happened when you went to Venice then? On your honeymoon. Did you find out anything about your mother?'

'In Venice I went to the address from which she had sent her letter to Camille. A man opened the door and there was a woman standing behind him. She was too old to be my mother. I don't speak Italian and they didn't understand me. The woman seemed sympathetic but the man didn't like me. I could tell he was the kind of man who would have been a fascist sympathiser when the fascists had the upper hand and a partisan sympathiser when they had the upper hand. I kept peering over his shoulder into the apartment. I was looking for some ghost of my mother. I understood while trying to make that man understand me why uneducated men resort to violence when arguing. The frustration of not being able to make plain what you mean makes you clench your fists. I didn't learn anything about my mother in Venice. The only times I enjoyed Venice were when I was able to imagine Ada was with me. Whenever I felt happy I wanted to share the moment with her. It didn't seem fair that she wasn't beside me, sitting on a wooden jetty by the side of the Grand Canal listening to the waves lap the pillars. I avoided your grand-mother. I found this little bar where there was a dwarf who played the slot machine. For some reason he didn't like me. It bothered me he didn't like me. He wasn't really a dwarf. Just short, as many Italian men are. I wondered if my rapist father was short.

'I remember once entering Piazza San Marco at some point towards sunrise. I had it all to myself. It was swept clean and seemed to have great expectations of me. I found myself wishing Ada could see me now. There was a kind of grandeur about the fact that I was the only person in the entire world who was standing on this historic stage. I felt as though I was being told a momentous secret but was too drunk and exhausted to understand it.

'My favourite occupation in life has always been talking to Ada. That's something that has never changed. I like it best when I can talk to her aloud. Which is one reason I've shunned company most of my life. I wish I could say that I don't care if people think I'm mad. But it's not true. I've spent a lot of my energy hiding how mad I might be from the general public. I've trained myself not to speak aloud to Ada when I'm outside the house though sometimes the odd phrase slips out. Out there in the world, it's like an assembly line. Everything has to run smoothly. And a lot of people like to think of themselves as the foreman. So if you act out of line you attract hostile attention. You're singled out and you become like a magnet for every escape of negative energy. And it's then you realise just how much negative energy there is out there swirling about, searching for a fix. It's like everyone knows how sensitive you've been made to feel and takes advantage of it to let off some of their own steam. So by the time you arrive home you feel like you've had the clothes ripped off your body. That's why I don't talk aloud to Ada in the streets. I just hope she doesn't think I'm being a coward again. Of course you think it's mad of me to believe Ada, who is dead and has been dead for many years, is any longer capable of thinking anything. But how do you know that for sure? We don't know anything for sure. Perhaps Ada is listening to us now. Perhaps all our spells would have had their desired effect had we carried them out. Perhaps this is all a long dream and I'll wake up tomorrow and find myself in a completely different world as a completely different being. You can't tell me for sure that won't happen.'

'So you keep your options open,' I said.

'So I keep my options open. Ada's silence became the new medium through which we might communicate. Except I've failed to crack the code, the enigma code. I can't access her messages. All the important moments of history I've shared with her. All the events she's missed. The times I've lived through belong as much to her as they do to me. This is her lifetime as much as mine. I shared news of the moon landings with her. I don't like to think of her not knowing about the important things that happen. We used to look at the moon together. Maybe we even devised a spell which would take us there. I couldn't feel the excitement of anything until I shared it with Ada. Or sometimes it would be the sadness I felt I had to share with her. Like when Martin Luther King was murdered. Such a beautiful and inspiring man. I knew Ada would have liked him. She always liked men whose hearts you could hear beating.'

'Now you're talking in the past tense,' I said. 'Does this mean you've stopped talking to her?'

'Past tense, present tense, future tense – what does it matter? When you reach my age they all become muddled anyway. Differentiating tenses - it's all just another form of housekeeping.'

'What about your mother? What about the dancer?'

'I'll tell you about her when we've crossed the English Channel. I want us to undertake a journey together. This is the favour I want to ask of you.'

His request brought me out in an immediate cold sweat. I succumbed to a moment of annoyance. By asking me to do something that was beyond me he was making me feel ashamed of myself. The last thing I wanted at this moment was to disappoint him.

19 Somehow the Wonder of Life Always Prevails

'When I was very crazy and believed the only way out was to kill myself I went to Virginia Woolf's house in Rodmell. The only books I read in those days were about the Holocaust or about famous people who had killed themselves. I have to feel some sort of personal connection when I'm reading a book. A book without personal connections to me is like a landscape without any living creatures.

'A lot of life and especially childhood is spent either grappling with a sense of injustice or fleeing from justice in the form of punishment. I believed there were many things I did that I deserved to be punished for. But what I did to Ada struck me as something punishable only by death. Perhaps in those days I *was* guilty of giving my guilt melodramatic airs.

'Anyway, I thought maybe Virginia Woolf's ghost might inspire me, might give me some tips. The thing that most surprised me about her suicide was how much time she gave herself to change her mind, to chicken out. She wrote her note but it's a long and potentially inspiring walk from her house to the River Ouse. I tried to imagine that walk. What she thought about. How many times she had second thoughts. What her eye was struck by. I couldn't help thinking of Ada's walk from the freight car to the gas chamber.'

Another synchronicity. I had been to Rodmell with Katie. Virginia Woolf was her favourite writer. She said *The Waves* was the closest literature had ever come to expressing the blueprint of dance which for her was mapping out and choreographing the secret springs of identity. Dance, she said, was making the inner life visible and giving it a sequential form. For her this was exactly what Pina Bausch did in her choreographies. The afternoon we went to Virginia Woolf's house was one of my favourite days with her. It was the first time she had driven me in her car outside London. I remember narrow lanes and tunnels of overhanging trees. The seemingly undisturbed peace of village life. We sat on a bench in Virginia Woolf's garden talking about marriage, imagining ourselves married and living in a house like that. There is something about that house and garden that makes marriage and domesticity bewitchingly attractive. Or it did to me. I remember we laughed about the irony of its atmosphere of exalted intimacy because, of course, one of the fundamental conditions for a happy marriage for Virginia was that there be no sex involved. Katie asked me if I'd still marry her if she imposed the same condition. I can't remember what I said. Except I realised she could probably renounce sex without much difficulty and perhaps even with some relief. Her relationship with her body, which she viewed as a finely tuned instrument to be maintained with scrupulous care, was a fastidious closely monitored affair. There were days when she ate nothing but carrots and apples. She couldn't pass glass without performing some snippet of choreography that she studied with critical intensity. She lived in front of mirrors. Practising spins and leaps. Circular walks with spiral twists. Falls and recoveries. She told me the most difficult challenge on stage was to dance without the constant partnership of her reflection. That the dancer is trained to enter the world of the mirror until it is no longer necessary to look. But that the mirror could trap a dancer's soul. I wasn't quite sure what she meant by that. Though sometimes when I touched her she seemed detached as though watching my fingers on her flesh from a point outside her body. Sometimes it seemed she kept her body embalmed in cellophane like a gift she was saving for a special occasion in the future. That special occasion didn't appear to involve my presence.

'I once heard a recording of Virginia Woolf's voice,' I told my grandfather. 'It was in the National Portrait Gallery. She sounded like one of those Tory politicians who strain to sound posher than they are. I couldn't reconcile that dry mannered voice with all the mischievous exuberance of *Orlando*. So Virginia Woolf didn't inspire you?'

'Actually she did. I found something in that garden, an echo of the atmosphere in our tree house which brought Ada back to me, the Ada I had known before I betrayed her. And I realised that if I was dead there would be no one to keep Ada alive. Did you know Virginia Woolf was buried underneath an elm tree in her garden? Of course that's no longer there. I've always found it extraordinary that elm trees, like dinosaurs, have completely vanished from the world. How can a whole species of tree cease to exist overnight? No wonder the past often seems fictitious. Irrelevant even. But then trees produce what enables us to preserve the past. How much less we'd know without paper. Maybe it'd be better to know less? But it's strange to realise how much communication trees have been responsible for. Every tree is a potential diary or love letter.'

'Or a gas bill, a parking ticket,' I said.

'Or a book of spells. Let's hope our tree wasn't an elm; let's hope it's still there,' he said, picking up a pencil and doodling on the back of his hand. 'It wasn't long after I said goodbye to Virginia Woolf that I realised there was one way I might see Ada again. I needed to speak to someone who knew about reincarnation. I was working in a nursing home when I had this revelation. You might have heard a woman there left me lots of money. I wouldn't have been able to get through life as I've lived it without that money. Your grandmother thought I was her toy boy. But Mrs Sopwith didn't leave me the money because she particularly liked me. She left me the money to infuriate her son who she always complained about. And sure enough it infuriated him. He used to park outside my flat and just sit inside his car for hours. I'm not one to call the police. I've never held much store in calling on officialdom to legislate my feelings. This man though was beginning to unnerve me. Another woman in the nursing home had several times mentioned a cult her granddaughter belonged to. I heard the cult was founded on a belief in reincarnation. That was like an annunciation. I worked out, perhaps erroneously, that, given the amount of time it takes a soul to pass from one body through bardo to another, Ada would be eleven years younger than me. That struck me fine as an age gap. And if anyone could tell me where Ada was now living it was Guru, the founder of this cult or community. Maybe you think reincarnation is a daft idea but I'd say it's important to believe in the immortality of the soul even if you don't believe in it, even if your mind rejects the idea as far-fetched, because it's crucial in life to establish what deserves our loyalty and there's no better measure of that than the concept of immortality. If reincarnation is true no life gets cut short. Nothing of meaning counts for nothing. Everything is continued.' He was up on his feet performing a pantomime Egyptian dance. I gave him the reward of a grin.

20 Words with the Shaman

'The community was like a world unto itself. It was virtually self-sufficient. There were all manner of farm animals and several vegetable gardens, as well as fields of grain and an apiary. It consisted of several farm buildings, most of which were converted into dormitories. I think about seventy people lived there. You could tell just by looking at these people that none of them liked football. They were competitive amongst themselves, all courting Guru's favour. The contest took the form of demonstrating in the most ostentatious fashion to what extent ego had been conquered. Therefore they fought among themselves for the most demeaning jobs. Everyone wanted to clean the latrines. It was easy to imagine Guru secretly allowing himself a wry mischievous smile.

'All religious ceremonies were respected, be they Hindu, Buddhist, Christian, Islamic or Judaic. There were countless services every day. The first one started at five in the morning. A man called Brother Andrew was allowed to take Catholic Mass even though he had never been ordained as a priest. He was also called upon to libate many of the sacred images in milk, honey, curd and ambrosia.

'Every day, beginning at four-fifteen in the morning

when the gates of the ashram would be opened, coaches and cars would arrive filled with day-trippers, pilgrims and people with sicknesses. The terminally ill were allocated "care houses". I was told for many people Guru was the last hope of a cure. I don't think he approved of cures though. Everything was karma. Whatever happened to you was warranted – it was part of the growing body of knowledge you would need to take into your next life. I gathered that he was able to remember his last five lives. He even had an old sepia photograph of himself in his last reincarnation – he was a Tibetan monk whose grave had become a holy shrine. 'Silly people don't realise I'm still alive,' he was reported to have joked once.

'By far the most picturesque feature of the place was the elephant. She had been flown over from Sri Lanka at great expense. She had a Hindu name which I forget but was nicknamed Lulu. She was used for pageants and ceremonies, dressed in a multi-coloured coat strung with tiny bells.

'One day I had set up my easel with the intention of painting her. I can't paint. I have no talent. But I like the act. It reminds me of our spell book. The way it heightens concentration to a sharp pitch. I like to think of each picture I paint as a spell. And I paste my pictures into a book. I can show them to you if you like. But not now. So there I was with my watercolours when I became aware of an agitation in the air. I looked up in time to see Lulu swing her trunk at my easel. She then stamped on it for good measure and looked at me with a kind of twinkle in her eyes. Guru, who was a squat ageless man with great reserves of energy, made a joke about Lulu being an astute art critic. She was notoriously mischievous. Twice she locked Father Eric in the barn – employing a deft dexterity of trunk and tusk to bring down the bar and twist a handle into its locking position. Father Eric was her carer and slept with her in the barn. She unzipped his sleeping bag at night. She would unzip it and then zip it back up again. I was told she had eaten his watch and his torch on countless occasions – they always still worked when they came out the other end a couple of days later.

'Guru himself was predominantly flirtatious. He spoke in a playful bantering tone which was extremely attractive. He didn't speak very often of his beliefs, at least not to me. He flirted. He had the ability to change his personality to suit the person at hand. If you were diffident and taciturn he would lower his eyes and protectively hug himself. If you were brash and outgoing he would use expansive gesture and raise his voice. He also had an eerie way of mimicking your facial expressions. And in this way he made you aware of certain traits within yourself. He showed me my vanity – and made me realise I am vain about my failings rather than my quali-ties. I asked him once if he remembered me from another life. He pretended to sweep his hand through his hair exactly as I realised I often did. Guru often winked at me whenever I asked him a question. I'm still very fond of him. After Ada he's perhaps the person who most haunts me. Haunts me with goodwill.

'The first time I saw Penelope she was looking at the bronze statue of Vishnu which stood by the side of one of the pathways near the lake. The Hindu god of preservation was reclining amongst the coils of a seven-headed cobra. There was a smell of incense in the air and the sun was setting over the hills which enclosed the community. Penelope had arrived at the community by mistake. Welsh names can be confusing. She had been expected at a house party in a village which shared many of the same letters as the place which housed the community. The taxi driver at the local station didn't listen closely to her confusion. He simply nodded his head and told her to get in. He was used to lost souls wandering dazed out of the station. He automatically took each and every one of them to the monastery.

'Penelope immediately attracted me. Very rarely did women attract me. When I heard the story of how she arrived at the ashram I decided it was fated that Penelope and I should meet. This in itself made her a plausible candidate as Ada's reincarnation in my eyes. She was there for a full moon ceremony in May. Relics inside gold caskets were exposed on this day – grey bone fragments belonging to Buddha and his disciples apparently. They were all tied with pieces of wire. I was told they grew year by year and that the tiny pieces of bone even multiplied. There was an air of great excitement before opening the caskets for this reason. Something about this ceremony reminded me of our book of spells. The evidence began to seem to me incontrovertible.

'It was on the day of the opening of the caskets that Penelope and I sat up talking by the lake beneath the full moon. I gave her my tweed jacket to wear and was pleased by how well it suited her. We were called upon to make sense of her mistaken arrival at this place where there were fragments of Buddha's bones in caskets, an elephant, gaunt individuals wandering around in robes and the elaborate statue of the Hindu god behind us. I told her it was as if large forces had conspired to bring about our meeting. I don't think she shared my point of view. She changed position on the ground and I caught a glimpse of her black knickers inside the folds of her skirt. Again I was reminded of Ada, of all the times I had caught glimpses of her knickers and her bare thighs. Penelope told me she had to be getting back to her quarters. I had the feeling she had seen me steal that glance along the inside of her thigh and this was her response. I knew I frightened her and because Ada was never frightened of me I knew she wasn't Ada.

'We were individually reprimanded the next day. Brother Peter was my inquisitor. He told me it was against the rules to fraternise with members of the opposite sex; that the monastery was not an amusement park. That night I crept away from the main building towards the woods. I think it was the pinprick glow of my cigarette that gave me away. Smoking was forbidden. Brother Peter seemed to materialise out of the thick darkness in one abrupt instalment. He shone a torch on me. He looked murderous in his black robes. Like an apparition from a medieval century. Penelope also got into more trouble the next day when it was discovered she had entered one of the temples while menstruating. I think most of the brothers and sisters were glad to see the pair of us leave. Not that we left together.'

21 A Dream Within a Dream

'I knew nothing more about my mother until I read a certain book. There was a time when I couldn't stop reading about the Holocaust. It was like one of those lessons at school when no matter how many times an equation is explained you still can't grasp the internal logic which allows you to file it away and move on to the next problem. Maybe I lived in hope of coming across Ada's name or a photograph of her. Certainly I felt a need to piece together every step of the journey she was forced to undertake after we were separated. I read about the two camps in France where she was held. I learned she was initially held in a camp at a place called Beaune-la-Rolande. Her parents and everyone else over twelve years of age were quickly put on a transport. The children were left behind, separated from their parents and more or less made to fend for themselves. They had no beds, no change of clothes and were barely given any food. Grown men were guarding these children. French gendarmes. I wonder what these men now say when their grandchildren ask them what they did in the war. I went to this camp. There was nothing left of it. Needless to say, the French aren't very keen to publicise that part of their heritage. The station is still there though. Weeds and nettles growing between the rusted rails. The silence of the place was almost visible. I stood on the platform and shut my eyes. There's a museum now somewhere near. I want us to go there after Paris. Apparently there are lots of photos of the children and a plaque. I'm not sure I want to see a photograph of Ada but I want you to see her. I want you to keep her alive now. It'll help if you can put a face to her. You still don't think you're coming, do you? But I know you better. You will come.'

I knew I would have to tell him why I wouldn't be able to accompany him. I was breaking out in a cold sweat just imagining myself on an aircraft. Trapped in a metal canister for at least an hour, breathing in pressurised air, squashed in with people in death poses. The thought of how much panic my mind might generate in that imagined hour terrified me. Like I said before, it's the fear of fear which is debilitating.

'Actually, perhaps I do want to see a photograph of Ada. Perhaps I'll see something there that will help me forgive myself for what I did to her.

'I eventually went to Auschwitz. It took me many years to muster up the resilience. Something else I did that was used against me as evidence of my unstable state of mind. A psychiatrist once made me drop my trousers and pants. He then told me I wasn't Jewish and asked me why I appeared to believe and act as though I was Jewish. He came up with various theories why he thought I was obsessed with the Holocaust. He often tried to assure me I had nothing to feel guilty about. Caring too much can seem like and even develop into illness but not caring a damn damns you to perdition without you realising it. I didn't tell him I wanted to see what Ada saw just before she died. That I wanted to walk over the stretch of the earth where she lived the last moments of her life and drew her last breath. I wanted to leave my footprints where she had left her last footprints. The remains of the camp should have heralded a vision. But I was struck by how mundane it looked, like an abandoned factory. I had to use my imagination and all the images that had branded themselves on my mind's eye from books. I turned the day into night. I saw the wash of dazzling white light when the freight car door was unbolted and slid open. I heard the army of dogs snarling, the shrieking of whistles. I saw the watchtowers and the high flicker of flame through the wash of smoky white light in the near distance. Ashes falling more quickly than they could be brushed away. I imagined Ada experiencing this moment of arrival. I imagined her using our spell to make herself invisible and for a moment I saw her slipping unnoticed past all the dogs straining on their leashes, pawing the air, past all the crying children and the bewildered mothers with matted hair, past the Nazi doctors in their white coats, the SS men in their tall boots with their riding whips. Then I imagined her fear when she realised the spell hadn't worked. I imagined her blaming me for the spell not working. I was sure she would have thought of me at least once and that therefore she had brought me to this hell on earth. I had had an existence here, albeit only as a thought. When I looked at all the shoes in the glass cases I kept expecting to see her sandals. When I looked at all the other artefacts I kept expecting to see our book of spells. I kept expecting to have the breath knocked out of me. Where is that book? Is it still somewhere out there in the world? There were photos of me and Ada together stuck on its pages. Did she take it with her to Auschwitz? Or did she leave it behind for the Nazis to take away? I have a feeling I now know where it is. And that's the chief reason we're going to Paris.

'A few weeks ago I realised I was little more than a tired ageing man of no consequence. Then I thought of you. Realised there'd be no such thing as you if it weren't for me. A banal thought but it struck me like a revelation.

'Anyway this book I mentioned is called *Six Italian Jewish Families and the Holocaust*. Can you imagine what it felt like for me to read my mother's name in a book? I think my heart stopped beating. I kept rereading her name. I couldn't get beyond it. My entire being refused to advance to the next sentence. I remember once reading that Virginia Woolf couldn't step beyond a puddle because she was suddenly so overcome by the strangeness of life. That's how I felt. I felt if I read on I would be annihilated. I had to put the book down. I went out into the garden and discussed the shock with my friend.'

'The mannequin?'

'I call him François,' he said, with his most charming self-effacing smile. 'It took François almost an hour to convince me to carry on reading. My mother worked for OVRA. That's the fascist secret police. The Italian equivalent of the Gestapo. She was an agent. Agent 762. In 1932, little more than a year after she gave me up, she infiltrated a group of communists and subversives at the university of Venice. She wrote reports, some of which apparently still exist today, in her handwriting. The book though wasn't interested in her activities during this time. This was included as a footnote of biographical information. She made the pages of this book because of something she did during the war years. It was her who denounced members of one of the Jewish families this book chronicles. A husband, wife and their ten year old son. The son was the same age as me. If she gave me away she did something much worse to this little boy. They were all murdered at Auschwitz. She was the only example in the book of an Italian national denouncing any Jew. On the whole it appeared Italians were generous in the help they provided Jews. My mother was an exception. I now had the two most important branches of my family tree. My father was a rapist and my mother a Nazi snitch.'

'Perhaps surrendering you up traumatised her so much she lost her mind?'

I was thinking of Katie and how much damage, in my eyes at least, the abortion had done to her ability to connect feeling and thought as one unified force.

'My guess is, she did the spying for the money. She wanted above all to go to America to study with some dancer there. That was her justification for giving me up. This is what Camille implied without actually saying. Therefore she had to do it, she had to go to America to exonerate her decision.'

'But she never went to America.'

'I don't know that. Maybe she did. Maybe she wasn't good enough to study with this dancer? There are only two moments of her life that interest historians and have been documented. That she was a secret agent working for the fascist secret police and that she denounced a Jewish family to the Nazis. The rest is all a mystery. I wrote to the author of this book. I told him Elisa was my mother. I heard nothing back. I expect he thought I was a crank. The letter I wrote him embarrasses me now when I think of it. I was used to conversing with François, a showroom dummy. I wasn't very good at addressing real people. But then he did write back. Two months ago in fact. He told me he had learned something new about my mother since writing the book. He gave me the telephone number of someone he said I should speak to. I don't like the telephone. That's why I don't have one. And I was frightened of talking to this person. I wasn't sure I wanted to hear what he might have to say. Every day I put off making this call. Until the day before yesterday.'

'What did this person say?'

'He was American which caught me off guard. I was expecting a muddled conversation in pidgin English. He told me I needed to speak to his wife. That she wasn't in Venice at the moment but she soon would be. He said I ought to come to Venice and speak to her. I can't concentrate on telephones at the best of times. I'm too agitated to concentrate on what's being said to me. I expect I sounded rude. It can't be helped now. I suppose if you dwell too much on the dead as perhaps I do you come to share their estrangement. Perhaps I've lived too long without any fresh counsel.'

'François doesn't come up with any nuggets of wisdom then?' I said, nodding towards the window. Not that I could see the mannequin through the thick drapery of foliage.

'He manages the border between this world and the beyond. He's the threshold guardian. Anyway, this man gave me his address and told me his wife would be happy to tell me everything she knew about my mother. And that's why we're going to Venice.'

My skin prickled. I was imagining myself on that aircraft again. I was about to invent some excuse. But he had confided so much of his secret life to me it felt miserly not to tell him the real reason why I couldn't go to Paris or Italy. I had never spoken to anyone about my terror of feeling trapped in an enclosed space with strangers. It was such a deep source of shame. The humiliation I felt was like when no one talks to you at a party and the empty space around you expands until it feels you're isolated in a different dimension.

'I've got this problem,' I said, steeling myself against the disdain I believed my affliction warranted. I offered my grandfather a cigarette. He was looking at me with more interest than he had yet shown me today. 'Call it a phobia,' I said, hating the scant banality of the word. 'I can't travel on public transport,' I said. 'A panic attack arrives as soon as the doors shut me in. Imagine what a bird would go through in a second class train carriage – that's what I go through, except unlike a bird, I have to contain and conceal the panic while every impulse of my mind and body is urging me to openly dramatise it.'

'You might have got that from me, I'm sorry to say. My mind has a predilection for anarchy. I'll tell you something, something I learned during the war years. Nothing makes a person more untrustworthy than to be motivated primarily by fear.'

'Yes, I've discovered that,' I said.

'You don't like closed doors?'

'I don't mind doors as long as I can open them with my own hands. When you were speaking about reincarnation I had this idea,' I said. 'The memory of someone who had been locked inside a cattle truck with a scrum of terrified people pissing and shitting themselves would flood the kind of panic I experience through the system every time they subsequently found themselves locked in a confined space with other people. Perhaps it's some kind of atavistic memory that is activating all this anarchy in my head? It's the first time I've felt a visceral connection to what the Jews went through.'

He nodded. I could tell he wasn't listening, that he was thinking ahead. 'What about a car?' he said. 'Could you travel in a car?'

'You can't drive. I can't drive.'

'Another thing we have in common. We'll go in a taxi then.'

I couldn't help laughing. 'To Italy?'

'Why not?'

I found I could just about imagine myself in a taxi.

'I'll think about it,' I said, still convinced I would say no. 'Anyway, I've got to go,' I said.

'Go where?'

'Home.'

'The halfway house?'

I nodded. 'There's something on TV I want to watch.'

He was offended. I was still very much a child with adults. I rarely enjoyed the demands they made on my time. I was always impatient to wind up every conversation and return to my own world. So I marvelled at the ease and pleasure with which I had settled into my grandfather's company today. Barely once had I succumbed to a fit of fidgets since arriving. It upset me that I had offended him.

'It's a documentary about Pina Bausch. She's a dancer. I've been looking forward to it for weeks. My ex-girlfriend might be in it. That's why it's so important to me.'

'Let's watch it together. I'd like to see her.'

I thought about this. It would mean walking back to the hostel in the witching hour. I knew from experience that hiking through London's streets around midnight was a gauntlet of perils. Once I was punched in the face without provocation. Luckily the three youths found no impulse to inflict further humiliation on me. They walked off, laughing.

'You've got a TV?' I said.

'Not here, no. But there's a shop in the high street. Electrical appliances. They always leave the TVs on at night.'

'We stand outside the shop watching it?'

'Why not?'

Because I still felt I had to refuse to accompany him on the grand tour of his past I felt compelled by guilt to agree to this request. Inwardly though I was cursing my compliance.

22 Imitation of Christ

It was dark when we left his house. He looked up at the sky, studying it as if trying to read his horoscope up there.

'I don't think Ada and I ever believed for one moment that the stars are deaf,' he said. 'Or not until her parents were taken from her at the French transit camp. Later that night I'm sure she felt the stars were deaf.'

A scruffy dog, as if magnetised, came ambling towards us, eyes riveted to my grandfather's face, tail wagging fervently. Then I saw the homeless man in the shop doorway. He looked up at us from under his eyebrows. Then gave my grandfather a series of coded nods.

'My grandson,' my grandfather said with an abruptness that verged on appearing rude, as if he was expected else-where at any moment and had no time to waste.

The bearded man eyed my grandfather as if he had just made a perplexing move in a game. 'This kind man gives me money every night but this is the first time he's ever spoken to me,' he said to me. He had a high-pitched querulous voice. I smiled uncomfortably. 'Not that I'm complaining. Far from it. He's saved my bacon many a time. And Spike always knows that when he appears she'll get a treat. That's why there's such a shine in her eyes.'

'I want to ask you a question,' my grandfather said, school-ing himself to speak more slowly. I could tell how much effort it was costing him to appear like a rational well-meaning member of the general public. In that moment I realised how little my grandfather had adapted himself to the conventions of social interaction; how little he emulated the behaviour of other people. As a result he lacked authority out in the world. He was not, like my father, a man who felt enlarged when he heard the national anthem. It was as if only his own achieve-ments played a part in his self-esteem, not those of king and country. As if tradition to him was like the furniture he had removed from his house. There was still something of the shy feral child in him.

'How did I end up sleeping rough, you mean?' He kept smiling up at me rather than at my grandfather. I could sense this new direction his relationship with my grandfather was taking troubled him. As if a silent contract they had enjoyed was in the throes of being torn up. He had sores on his lips and dirt was as if tattooed on his face, neck and hands.

'I want to know if you can you drive a car?'

'A car? If I had a car I could drive it. More chance of a meteor striking the planet than me acquiring a car though.' He smiled up at me again.

'How would you feel about me buying you a car? On one condition. You drive my grandson and me to Paris and then to Italy? I'll pay you. How about two hundred pounds a day plus expenses?'

'Is there a hidden camera somewhere?' The man offered an uncertain wave at a space behind our heads. There was a hint of affronted malice in his amusement as if he suspected my grandfather was making a monkey of him. 'Am I on television? This is a practical joke, right?'

'I'm serious. As long as you have a driver's licence.'

The man, who still hadn't stood up, who still sat huddled in the heavy shadow of the doorway, rummaged in the inside pocket of his filthy jacket. Another face came through his beard as he held up his credentials. Excitement widened his eyes at the same time as resentment, as if fearing himself duped, sucked in his mouth. 'There you go. One driving license.'

'Think it over. Paris and Italy,' said my grandfather, still appearing awkward, like a novice on skis.

'You're pulling my leg. You must be pulling my leg. Is he pulling my leg?' he asked me.

'We should go,' I said to my grandfather. 'The documentary will be starting soon.'

'Think it over,' my grandfather said.

'I'd have to bring Spike,' he said, pulling his dog closer and stroking its matted fur. 'If you're not pulling my leg that is.'

'No problem,' my grandfather said.

What did he mean, no problem? Dogs had to be quarantined before being allowed into a foreign country, didn't they? I knew both relief and disappointment in the evidence now before me that my grandfather's plan would doubtless never get off the ground.

'Every day I feel guilty for not offering that man a room in my house,' my grandfather said as we walked away. 'It's empty after all. I keep trying to find a polite way of telling him he's welcome to stay with me as long as I don't have to speak to him or see him. But I can't find a polite way of expressing these conditions.'

'Sometimes we just have to turn the other cheek,' I said, disliking but unable to see beyond my cynicism.

23 Methods of Dance

We had arrived at the electrical appliance store. None of the televisions in the brightly lit window were tuned to BBC 2.

'No problem,' my grandfather said. And he led me further down the street.

A man with thinning black hair was sitting behind the counter craning his neck up at a small television perched high on a shelf. A hospital drama. Men in green bibs and bonnets putting broken people back together again. This did not augur well. The last time I was face to face with a hospital drama all the rules of my reality changed. The man jumped to his feet and smiled when he saw my grandfather. I got the idea my grandfather almost single-handedly kept Fungsun Express in business. The man, with only quirky broken English at his disposal, seemed braced to misunderstand whatever was said to him. In fact, it wasn't easy for my grandfather to explain to him what exactly we required – two portions of shrimp fried rice and the television switched over to BBC 2.

Thus it was that I watched the Pina Bausch documentary with my grandfather in a Chinese takeaway. When Katie appeared on the screen I stared first in wonder, then in jealousy. I was jealous she had travelled so far without me.

'That's her,' I told my grandfather. 'That's Katie.'

'That's her,' my grandfather told the man behind the counter. The man smiled politely. I could imagine him later, perhaps in bed with his wife, using me and my grandfather as another anecdote of British eccentricity.

There was a brief clip from a choreography called *Palermo Palermo* in which Katie, wearing stilettos, was dancing an impassioned argument with a male dancer. An ugly emotion rendered beautiful by the stylised gestures the dancers made of their bodies. I was jealous of the male dancer, the eloquence with which his body expressed urgent feeling. If only I had met Katie's argument with such grace and bewitchment. Every movement seemed inevitable when she danced, like ink forming letters into words on paper, but there was also a primitive power in the medley of shapes her body made. I was dismayed how short the clip was. Over as soon as it began. It seemed an awful and unfair impoverishment that I wasn't allowed to watch the entire performance. Was that really so much to ask for of life?

There was now a lengthy interview with Pina Bausch. She was sitting in a chair, chain smoking. Her elegant hands danced while she spoke. My grandfather turned to me and told me he liked the look of Pina Bausch. 'She wouldn't have joined the Nazi party,' he said. Then there was Katie again, her black hair loose, barefoot in a long sherbet pink dress. The stage was awash with water. Katie kicked and splashed about in it while male dancers threw buckets of water at her. Drenched, she flopped down onto the wet floor and began making crab-like movements, scuttling backwards on her hands and feet over the wooden boards with a kind of primitive grace. I watched the shifts in the thin silk of her skirt against her thighs, the lightness with which her bare feet skimmed the floor. I had never seen her look more bewitching. This was not the idealistic self-regarding virtuosity of classical ballet conducted on tip-toes in rarefied air; this was a naked grounded celebration of the human form battling with its own pivotal elements, a transfiguration of the human spirit's susceptibility to fall and recovery. It was strange to see her picked out by a spotlight on the stage. It was how I always saw her nowadays, distinct and set apart from the rest of life.

'I enjoyed that,' my grandfather said. He touched me on the shoulder. I saw the vein for taking pleasure was still youthful and eager in him. I was moved by the interest he showed in Katie. His appreciation consecrated my feeling for her. He made me feel very proud of her and by reflex proud of myself as if I had played a part in her creation but also bereft for the fact of having lost her.

He insisted on giving me money for a taxi before I left. I had been unemployed for years, scrimping by on my paltry benefit payments. Rarely did I have enough money to grant myself a treat. Therefore, despite my apprehension about the perils awaiting me on London's streets at night, the imagined fist coming out of the dark, I couldn't bring myself to lavish this windfall on the luxury of a taxi. That money could buy me a book or some new music. I missed that satisfying feeling of carrying home something I had chosen to own.

24 Running up the Hill

There was an air of a storm arriving. The moon appeared to have speeded up its orbit as it gallivanted through a scrum of black clouds. I remembered another stormy night when Katie had flung open the windows of her bedroom. The wind began whipping the white muslin curtains into wild, exuberant yet anchored shapes. To my mind there was something sexual in the cavortings of the two separate veils of material. Like the doomed expression of the yearning to coalesce of two separate spirits. Katie though saw it as the exhilaration the body is capable of when all its energy is channelled into the pursuit of transcendence. Which, she said, is what dance was. I admired her dedication but I was jealous of it too. For one thing it was more intellectually formulated than any passion of mine. While I was in the band I had to prepare myself for the inevitable interview with a music journalist when I would be called upon to articulate some kind of manifesto behind our music. Everything I came up with sounded either pompous or trite. My instinct has always been to avoid all kind of earnest statements. Like 'I love you'. I never said those words to Katie. I now realised with an inrush of admiration that my grandfather had strung together a narrative of earnest statements this evening without coming across as trite or pompous. He had returned as a role model and mentor as he had been during my childhood

I was glad when it began raining. The rain minimised the odds of meeting a group of bored thugs for whom I might represent a moment of pleasure, the pleasure of accruing power by exploiting my weakness. Males in groups are dangerous when they have been made to feel powerless. These kind of males often patrolled the streets at night. I had mapped out this walk in my mind before setting out earlier. The length of Canon Street, passing St Brides and St Pauls, Fleet Street, The Strand, past the National Portrait Gallery and the National Gallery, into the Mall, past the ICA where my band had played a month or so after I left, across Green Park to Hyde Park Corner, across Hyde Park to Kensington High Street and the length of Kensington Church Street. Now I had to do it the other way round. Often I felt like a ghost on these long walks across London, returning to all the locations where I had been happy in another life.

I soon discovered I was greatly enjoying my long walk. I had found support and rest in my grandfather's company. And he had given me a lot to think about. He had also, in tandem with the BBC documentary, brought Katie closer. In Hyde Park, where the great stretches of blackened open space pin-pricked with distant lights took on something of the infinite, I knew a moment of exhilaration. I felt myself in perfect harmony with the world around me. I was overwhelmed by a feeling of having momentary escaped from the snares of my land-owning little ego. Of being exempt from the touch of time. The illusion of peace drifted me above and beyond the boundaries of time for a moment. Time had become a much more pressing enemy since the automated presumptions necessary for daily functioning began breaking down in me, since my time of innocence had ended. Here, in Hyde Park, I felt I was stealing a moment from time. And this stealing of moments from time was the only possibility of happiness now open to me. Probably the only possibility of happiness open to any of us. I felt I had momentarily achieved a feeling that represented me as I aspired to be represented. Though I was alone I felt intimate with everyone who was important in my life. As if they were close, watching me. I liked this idea. I thought this moment ought to be televised. That everyone I had ever known should now be able to see me as I walked across Hyde Park in the light rain, to feel my presence. As if they would feel the full force of the affection they felt for me if they could see and experience me at this moment.

Footlights lit up the old stones of the Tower of London, making it seem to float on a becalmed tide of darkness. I enjoyed the tiredness of my muscles, as if I had been engaged in fruitful physical labour all day. I felt oddly proud of myself when I greeted the receptionist at the hostel. For once the interrogation-room brutality of the fluorescent strip-lighting and the pervasive smell of animal fat and industrial detergent had no power to oppress me.

25 Nightporter

I shared a room at the hostel with a boy called Cedric. We were both uncomfortable with this arrangement for a while. Every piece of furniture except the sink by the window was duplicated. You saw double everywhere you looked which, at times, led me to think of Cedric as a kind of symbolic twin. An alternate version of myself in a parallel universe. There was a mosaic of postcards of painted Holy Virgins bluetacked above his bed. One of the first things he told me was that he had seen *Death in Venice* twenty-seven times. Katie and I had seen that film at The Scala in Kings Cross, my favourite cinema in London.

Cedric had bleached hair which would have wriggled into dainty curls had he not religiously had it cut very short every two weeks. He touched his clothes with reverent delicacy as if they were made of papyrus from ancient Egypt. His nightshirt was green and white and patterned with pictures of frogs. These frogs had the kind of human faces a child might draw. In his frog nightshirt and white woollen socks he would stamp off to the bathroom before going to bed. The corridors resounded with his footsteps. He walked heavily for someone so embarrassed by his physicality. The hostel was inhabited mainly by young males from deprived backgrounds who looked as though they used industrial detergents on their skin instead of shower gel. They hung around the corridors with cans of beer, making a raucous song and dance of their masculinity. They had mock fights, throwing pretend punches at each other while the fire alarm went off yet again. I was always curious what took place when they caught sight of Cedric stamping along beneath the fizzing fluorescent tubes in his frog nightshirt and white socks. I suppose if the truth be told it cost me some embarrassment to realise most of the hostel's tenants assumed Cedric and I were lovers. At the same time it seemed to serve me right that I was being misrepresented in the world at large.

'I found out today my great grandfather was a rapist and my great grandmother worked for the Italian secret police denouncing Jews to the Nazis for the cash,' I told him when he asked if I had had a good night. He was heating a can of spaghetti hoops on top of the toaster. We never went down to the canteen for our meals. We both agreed that it wasn't a good idea to attract attention in this place. We made do with the toaster. I hadn't eaten a vegetable for about two years.

Cedric didn't know how to respond to my statement. I saw I had to give him a helping hand. I had to turn it into comedy before he could relax. One of the givens in our relationship was that I was the performer and he was the audience. The problem was I couldn't find a joke in my anecdote. Cedric had a thing about the Nazis. Or perhaps, closer to the truth, he had a thing about Dirk Bogarde dressed up as a Nazi. After *Death in Venice*, *The Nightporter* and *The Damned* were his two favourite films. I thought for a moment of telling Cedric I might be going to Paris and Venice even though I doubted this would happen. I found I was frightened of making the declaration aloud, as if, like an air raid siren, it would herald the advent of panic.

I found it difficult to sleep. As often happened in his sleep Cedric had pushed down his blankets and his nightshirt had rucked up. He always had a kind of three-quarter erection which the fluorescent lights in the block opposite would shine in on. His penis looked very much like my own. It was the same size, had the same air of adolescent innocence. There was a wistfulness about its clandestine excitement. Poor thing, I used to think, treated to so little pleasure. But then who was I to speak?

I wondered how representative of personality every man's erect penis was. Mine was slim, not very big. It had a nice harmonious line; it wasn't knobbed or bent or truculent looking like some of the pink and black cudgels I had seen in pornography. It didn't look haughty or even terribly confident in itself. It probably represented me quite well. Katie took little close interest in it. Viewed it with mistrust a lot of the time. As if it wanted to interfere with the regimented rituals the dancer in her put her body through. She used to tell me how her female friends spoke of sex as a kind of clandestine war with their mothers. That the inspiration behind performing taboo acts – anal sex, threesomes, lesbian sex, sex in public places - was a kind of competition among themselves, enjoyed more in the telling of it than in the act itself. And that it was as if they were keeping a running scorecard to indisputably prove they had ventured further within themselves in the quest for self-knowledge than their mothers had. It was their way of validating the upwardly mobile trajectory of evolution. Katie liked to maintain an air of being above her sexuality. I think I'm similar.

I called my mother the next day. I found I was nicer to her than usual. Less avid to find fault with her. I put it down to my grandfather's new influence. I did not have a good relationship with either of my parents. Nothing in their house ever looked like it was used or even touched. I didn't understand how anyone could think this was a good precept by which to live. How much money they spent in exchange for knowing so little. I left home at sixteen after an explosive argument. My father told me I'd be back within twenty-four hours. Thus effectively cutting off this option. My first night of liberation was a sordid affair. As things panned out I didn't speak to them for four years. I now asked my mother if her father had ever spoken to her about his childhood in Paris.

'His childhood in Paris?'

'Yes.'

'To be honest I know nothing about his childhood. I do know he tells fibs.'

'Haven't you ever asked him?'

'No. Come to think of it.' She must have sensed a current of disapproval reaching her over the line. 'You think that's odd? How many questions have you ever asked me about my childhood?'

'Not a single one,' I conceded. 'But you don't know for sure he didn't grow up in Paris?'

'No. He told me he wanted to talk to you. Was that what he talked about?'

'Yes,' I said. I still wasn't sure I believed in Ada.

Part Two

I Come Morning

By taking me back in my ancestry my grandfather's narrative, if he wasn't spinning yarns, had also pushed me with a lighted candle down towards the realms of my mind plunged in darkness from where all my anxiety originated. Or that's how it felt. I sensed I had a war to fight. I had become far too abject. This is when I began to realise I might not have any choice but to accompany my grandfather on his madcap mission. His odyssey was my Iliad.

My grandfather made up a bed for me in one of his empty rooms the night before our departure. He disappeared off to the shed. I had never been to Paris or Italy. For most people getting from one part of the world to another has become an essentially automated act. Perhaps they experience the odd bout of butterflies, a frisson of nervous energy. For me though it was as nerve-racking, perilous and unimaginable as it must have been in the 17th century. I tried to train myself not to think beyond the simple obligations of the moment. But my mind kept projecting nightmare scenarios – the car broke down in France or worse was attacked by carjackers and I was forced onto a crowded train. A new fear was that the craziness in my mind would urge me to throw myself off the deck of the ferry. In museums I sometimes now had to fight down a perverse urge to destroy some precious ancient artefact or an old master painting. My mind in its madness seemed infatuated with random acts of violence or self-harm. I was less and less sure about opening my mouth for fear and mistrust of what might emerge. I therefore had to convince myself there would be hiding places on the boat where I could escape the prying eyes of my fellow human beings and mother myself into a calm state of mind. I still doubted I could go through with it. And dreaded the humiliation of having to openly admit it. As often happened I became anxious about becoming anxious.

I couldn't sleep so I went out into the garden. The grass was silvered with dew. Everything was touched by stillness. Excitement seemed in the process of being hatched in the air. And I had that cleansing feeling that the world was only continuing because I was awake and bearing witness to it. There's no time of day that makes me believe more in the possibility of change. It can seem as though the slate has been wiped clean. You can exalt in the virgin atmosphere of the birthing of a new day. There had been no such thing for me as a new day for a long time. Some neurological glitch had occurred in my mind. By now I harboured little belief that it would ever correct itself. And yet today really was a new day. I walked over to François, the showroom dummy, and asked him, in French, how he was getting on.

My grandfather had given me a banded wad of French francs and a banded wad of Italian lira inside. The large crisp thin French bank notes looked to me like the romantic currency of cavaliers and pirates. As if they might purchase treasures far more exotic than anything available to British banknotes. They reminded me of the sense of high adventure they had produced in me when I went on a school trip to Boulogne. That in turn reminded me of the bag of ornate marbles I had acquired in the French port and then the excitement of playing with these new precious talismans. For a moment I recalled the moral defeat of losing one of my own favourites in a game. And realised every single prized possession of my childhood had either found its way into different hands or vanished without trace. It occurred to me that those marbles still existed somewhere in the world. I couldn't think of any way they might disintegrate.

Towards five in the morning my grandfather appeared with a small rucksack and a rusted and mud-caked shovel. He appeared more protective of this shovel than his bag. When I asked him what it was for he raised his comedian's eyebrows and told me to wait and see. His shirt was buttoned crookedly. There was reassurance for me to be had here. Clearly I wasn't the only one who was nervous. I had only seen him once since he told me about Ada and his mother and he had said the only thing that worried him now was that he might have a heart attack before our departure.

'Your heart has seen you through,' I said. It occurred to me there was a much deeper truth in what I said than I had meant.

I was feeling light on my feet. There were butterflies in

my stomach. So far though my mind was behaving itself. The beginning of an attack I always experienced as a swell lurching up from unseen depths, similar to the physical sensation of standing waist-high in the sea when there are no waves but all of a sudden the great body of water heaves itself up as if the planet has shifted a fraction on its axis. That was the signal for me that the nature of reality was about to terrifyingly change.

Strangely it was the nature of reality that was to change for my grandfather. After he had made us both coffee I saw there was a fever in his clouded blue eyes.

'I don't think I can go through with this,' he told me. He sat down on the stairs, hugging his shovel. I had expected it to be me who would be saying these words. I realised at that moment how vital this adventure had become to me if I was ever to escape the claustrophobic forsaken world I was living in. I realised I was excited rather than frightened. One big reason I was excited was that I had discovered Katie was touring Italy with the Tanztheater. My grandfather had refused to give me an itinerary of our trip. He made a facetious comment about the mania to forward plan everything in life. But I knew he planned to visit Venice to follow up this mysterious lead about his mother. At the right time my intention was to tell him about Katie and suggest we go to Castiglion Fiorentino to watch her dance.

I tried to give him a pep talk but he was adamant. He couldn't go through with it. It had been a foolhardy idea. Then the homeless man arrived with his dog. Our taxi driver, Josh. I was struck by his transformation. Gone was the beard and the matted dirty hair. He was clean shaven and wearing new clothes. I didn't like this new clean cut version as much as his former wild man look. He appeared more acquisitive, less acquiescent. I understood my grandfather had given him a lifeline too. A lifeline he was about to tug back. The good cheer on his face vanished when he saw my grandfather hugging a shovel on the stairs with tears running down his face.

'I'm sorry. We won't be needing your services,' my grandfather said. Josh stood with his mouth open, like a feeding fish. I realised Josh was giving himself time and this giving himself time was perhaps his most characteristic trait.

It took almost half an hour to talk my grandfather out of his change of heart. I noticed there was a tuft of thread on his check tweed jacket where a button was missing. The absence of that button was like a magnet for all the affection I now felt for him. Finally we set off through the near deserted early morning streets of west London. Josh told us he had been out on a practice run the day before. That he had driven to Brighton and back to get a feel for being behind the wheel again. My grandfather sat in the front seat. I was in the back with Spike. Truth be told, the presence of the dog irked me. I wasn't looking forward to customs. It would be my job to hide him. And guardians of criminal law always induced a feeling of guilt in me no matter how innocent I believed myself to be. I also knew from experience that to anyone who represented law and order I looked, in spite of my best efforts, like an individual willing and eager to commit infringements.

2 Let the Happiness in

I didn't like the way Josh drove. The nonchalant way he lightly nudged the wheel with one hand while resting his elbow on the open window. He seemed to be constantly admiring himself. Somehow he lacked the humility you would expect from someone who has lived on the streets.

I got more and more nervous as we approached Dover. But I decided this was only natural. I was surprised by how new everything looked to my incarcerated eyes, as if freshly minted. I hid Spike beneath a blanket as we drove towards the ferry with the white cliffs in sight. We were ushered aboard without problems. Josh surreptitiously remained in the hold of the boat to keep Spike company. I felt exhilarated on the deck of the ferry. The wind blew spray up into my face and I thought how brilliant the weather can be sometimes at expressing your feelings. I was so thankful my mind wasn't betraying me, that it was allowing me to enjoy this moment of liberation. The upside of my affliction was that when panic was expected but didn't arrive there was a vibrant freshness to the world that met my eyes. My capacity to marvel had greatly increased. My capacity for wellbeing too. My mind had become more absorbent, more porous.

Needless to say I was greatly relieved when we weren't stopped by customs. As Josh accelerated off the dock my grandfather began singing *La Marseillaise* at the top of his voice and slightly out of tune. It suited him somehow that he couldn't sing in tune. It was strange to hear him so eloquent in French. He appeared in a new light to me, as if he had dyed his hair. Only then did I realise he had grown up speaking another language. But not the language of his country of birth or his parents. The money he had given me for a taxi I had spent on a book about Paris during the Nazi occupation. What most shocked me was how many French Nazis there appeared to have been. I had spoken about this with my grandfather. He told me it was just as well Britain had never been invaded and we never found out how many British Nazis there were. 'Nazis aren't confined to one country or to one period in history,' he said. 'There are Nazis everywhere, waiting to come out of cupboards.'

When my grandfather stopped singing I noticed in the rear view mirror that Josh's smile was strained. His thin lips turned down at the corners. I had the feeling he inwardly disdained the eccentricity of my grandfather and found me foolish or mercenary in some secret way for indulging it. Was it, I wondered, odd or natural for someone who had lived on the streets to be so judgemental? When I tried to imagine what it felt like when a stranger dropped some coins into his cup I decided the person giving would probably feel a bit better about himself and the person taking, Josh, would feel a bit worse about himself.

The countryside soon opened up. I enjoyed the sensation

of feeling smaller under so much sky. As if the less important I felt myself to be the less power my mind possessed to distort reality. I asked Josh to stop the car. Everyone assumed I wanted to relieve myself but what I wanted was to feel French soil under my feet. Spike too battled his way out of the car. I watched him running in exuberant circles at the side of the busy road. A little fearful for his safety. Having secretly cursed him for causing unnecessary tension I now felt affection for him as if he had become a good luck charm. I liked the way he looked at me. It had been a long time since eyes had regarded me with such trusting eager affection.

I couldn't quite believe I was in France. This was another upside to my affliction. Simple achievements acquired epic proportions. Now I was standing on foreign soil I felt a sense of achievement such as I hadn't felt since the panic attacks arrived in my life.

I also couldn't believe how elated I was while drinking my first cup of French coffee at a motorway service station. I felt a wellbeing of companionship with my fellow brunching adventurers in this roadside retreat. It had been some while since I had been able to look upon strangers with affection. I understood my grandfather's longing to share his every moment of excitement with Ada because I wished Katie could see me, could share my excitement. Even though I knew what a meagre achievement it was in most people's eyes, I felt proud of myself, instead of ashamed of myself, for the first time in ages.

The unfamiliar language spoken by every signpost offered a promise of escape from everything that had become overfamiliar and demeaning to me. How simple solutions can be sometimes, I thought. As we motored on towards Paris I found myself thinking about Katie and the abortion. There were days when I regretted the lost child. It would have been an enduring guarantee that Katie was always part of my life. I pictured a little girl, like Ada. I imagined her holding my hand. I imagined the warm purring weight of her sitting astride my shoulders. Then I wondered if it might have been better had Ada, if Ada really existed, never been born? Was all the excitement and wonder and love she had known in her short life worth the horror she had to endure at the end? Given the choice I'm pretty sure I would have opted not to have been born. But then I thought of the devotion she had inspired in my grandfather and realised how much I would love to be remembered with such sustaining creative affection.

There had been other days when my self-esteem was so low that I was forced to admit I wasn't fit to have a child. Katie herself had used this as one of her arguments which hurt me at the time. Before the abortion I had always complacently considered myself an enlightened modern male, immune to all the old patriarchal conceits and insensitivities of my father and my father's fathers. All of a sudden Katie had typecasted me as yet another insensitive male, if not a closet misogynist. The first sign of canker in my sense of identity.

As the signposts for Paris became ever more frequent I told my grandfather about the abortion and the rift it caused between Katie and me.

'You didn't want the child but you made out you did?'

'I'm not sure I made out anything. I didn't want things

to end with Katie. Of that I was certain. But I no longer recognised her. It was my first ever experience of someone undergoing a radical change in front of my eyes. Until then I assumed no one ever changed much. My parents never changed. Essentially aren't we all like furniture? We get stained, our springs give up, the odd rip in the fabric appears but the essential shape remains. She changed her shape.'

I could sense Josh was listening closely to what I was saying. He kept catching my eye in the rear view mirror. I divined in him the wish for a third party ally to whom he could confide his true thoughts about what was going on in the car. I assumed these private thoughts he habitually shared aloud with Spike, not of course now possible without us eavesdropping. His silence sometimes seemed double glazed, as if he wanted no one to hear what he was thinking. His presence troubled me. Most of all the dislike I couldn't help feeling for him. I thought my antipathy towards him marked a shameful lack of generosity in me. But it was something I felt on the pulse.

'I suppose she was trying to rationalise a decision that plummeted her down to depths where reason doesn't reach. She's wanted to be a dancer since she was about five. That desire was pivotal to her identity. A child would have derailed that ambition. I saw all that. But sometimes now I wonder if it wasn't an elaborate unconscious plan on her part to get rid of me. Why did she get pregnant? She never had before. To my knowledge she was on the pill. She never told me she had stopped taking it.'

I could tell that my grandfather had a grin on his face

though he sought to hide it. He must have sensed I was affronted because he apologised. 'It's just that I was thinking how your story with Katie is like a continuation of my mother's story. You have to admit it's uncanny. Two aspiring dancers both threatened in their ambition by female biology. Two aspiring dancers who become ghosts. We've also both discovered that there's a world of difference between hurting someone with a truth and hurting them with a falsehood. The first can't perhaps be helped; the second can turn your world inside out if there's no chance to rectify it.'

'I think you've done more than enough penance,' I said.

'I expect Josh thinks the same about himself.'

We had been talking as if Josh wasn't there with the implication we wished he wasn't, never a very flattering state of affairs for the ignored party. It was an impulse of charity on the part of my grandfather to include him now. I could have told my grandfather that Josh had clearly had his fill of charity.

'I wish I knew what you were talking about,' said Josh.

'How have you fared in relationships with women?'

'Probably I would give myself a six out of ten. I'll tell you what gets me. The way women can turn everything round to make it your fault. In my experience when a woman betrays you she might look a bit sheepish at first but that doesn't last long. Pretty soon it's your fault. We men can never quite get it right where feeling is concerned. It's always slightly underdone or a bit on the burnt side.'

'You'll get back on your feet,' my grandfather said, touching Josh lightly on the arm. 'One thing I've learned is that it's a mistake to prioritise the comedy over the pathos of experience. Comedy might make you more friends but it won't help you remain friends with yourself.'

'That's very wise, Max,' said Josh, though I could tell this wasn't what he felt. Truth be told my grandfather could at times come across as a bit patronising, a bit pompous. His shyness with strangers seemed to deny him his sense of humour. I wasn't sure if my grandfather chiefly irritated or bemused Josh. I knew he didn't care much for me which is why I didn't like him.

'When are we going to learn why you bought a shovel?' I asked.

'I was curious about that,' said Josh. 'But then I'm curious about this whole trip.'

'Call it a trip down memory lane,' said my grandfather.

'The shovel?'

'I remembered something I had forgotten for years. Ada's father didn't only build her the tree house; he also created a hiding place for treasure underneath it. He dug an oblong in the earth, reinforced it with wooden panels and covered it with turf. We never used it. That's why I'd forgotten about it. But maybe Ada used it without my knowing. Maybe she hid the book of spells there when she was angry with me.'

'You're going to ask a stranger if you can dig up their garden?'

'I'm going to have to word that request carefully, aren't I? I've been practicing in my mind how I might go about it.'

'And how are you going to go about it?'

'I'll tell the person what happened to Ada,' he said, swivelling inside his seatbelt to face me. Sunlight struck out highlights on the faint stubble on his chin and cheeks. 'And I'll tell them she left no trace of her life behind, except what maybe is buried in their garden. Let's hope I have to deal with a woman. I'll be less sure of myself if I have to deal with a man.'

I was excited when we entered the suburbs of Paris. I couldn't remember a time when such ugly vistas had incited so much wonder in me. My grandfather had so successfully infected me with the spirit of his narrative that I was almost surprised not to see German tanks rumbling along the Paris streets, Wehrmacht soldiers on motorbikes and sidecars, huge billowing Nazi banners draped over the buildings. The world of Nazi jackboots and the yellow star. We drove down the busy wide boulevards until the river appeared.

'Look! Shakespeare and Company,' I said. My eye more attracted to the green shopfront and the stacks of books on its courtyard than to Notre-Dame. It was one of the places in the world that held a ghost of Katie.

'That's an imposter,' my grandfather said, indignant. 'And it's not in the right location.'

His directions to Josh became ever more indecisive. And as he struggled to find his bearings the atmosphere in the car became more tense. I could sense Josh was growing increasingly irritated with my floundering grandfather. And ensnared in the cataracts of Parisian traffic Josh no longer seemed so sure of himself.

When we finally found the right street my grandfather told Josh to wait by the car. I sensed he didn't like being given orders. That he had had enough of us for the time being.

'This is where Ada lived,' my grandfather said. It was probably the most momentous moment I had ever participated in. It struck me how innocent the building appeared of its history. As if nothing out of the ordinary had ever happened behind its walls. I couldn't help staring at the door and picturing the eleven year old Ada escorted out in the middle of the night by those emissaries of the Holocaust in their gendarme uniforms. The door was as effectively masked of its sinister secret as any human face is of the adventures and crimes of its owner. For a moment I forgot to look at my grandfather. I was deeply curious about what was going on inside him. If I still had any lurking suspicion that he had fabricated the entire Ada narrative it was dispelled by the dazed look on his face. He stared up at one particular window. The expression on his face was one of blanched disbelief as if it was a miracle this place still existed in the world. I felt privileged that I was sharing such a pivotal landmark in my grandfather's history. It was like some essence of the wonder and sadness of my grandfather's childhood was streaming through time and waves of it now broke over our feet.

My grandfather had charm in abundance. It was probably the only social credential he did have. I couldn't help adopting a bemused apologetic air while he was explaining himself to the woman who opened the door. He was holding his shovel which clearly alarmed the woman. I've forgotten most of the French I learned at school so I only understood the odd word he said. The woman's face grew increasingly more engaged and troubled by what he was saying. When he delivered up the word Auschwitz she looked at him with a mixture of pity, disbelief and hostility. There was a moment of tension.

Then she opened the door wider. We entered the echoing vestibule. My grandfather was lavish with his thanks. I felt bad for not having quite believed in Ada. Then I tried to imagine what he was going through as we entered the building he hadn't seen for almost sixty years.

When the woman led us out into the garden my grandfather tottered and then sat down on the grass.

'The tree is in the wrong place,' he said, more to himself than to anyone else. There was a catch in his voice. It sounded like the recording of a voice from an old radio set, surrounded by a wasteland of static. I don't think I've ever seen anyone look so disbelievingly at what he saw. I too looked at the tree. I wish I knew what kind of tree it was but I was never taught anything about trees at school. Only chestnuts can I recognise because I spent some of my childhood throwing missiles up at them to dislodge conkers. The woman asked him if he was all right; she asked me if he was all right. I only possessed a few broken words in this foreign tongue with which to formulate an attempt at an answer and felt wholly inadequate to the situation at hand.

My grandfather looked like someone who has just woken up but is still inside his dream. All the phantasmagoria of his present situation swept through me in a single forceful gust. That he possessed living images in his mind of details I had only witnessed on the television, at the cinema – the Nazi flag, the yellow star – made me think of the gulf between the experience of the astronauts who had walked on the moon and all the rest of us for whom the moon is a far blown enigma.

The same enormous divide now materialised between my grandfather and me. For a moment he appeared ancient and not a little uncanny, like a ghost.

It was some while before he began digging. He looked terrified, as if on the verge of uncovering a corpse. Up until now I had thought this his most absurd idea but as he gently removed the first layer of soil excitement took hold of me. I felt like Schliemann monitoring his excavators as they searched for Helen's jewels. I've rarely wished for anything with such intensity as I wished his and Ada's book of spells would be buried in that earth. Before long a man appeared at a window and began shouting at us in French. When I looked back at my grandfather tears were streaming down his face. He had uncovered the hiding place. The oblong of wooden slats was still in place but the space it protected was empty.

As we were walking back to where the car was parked I said, 'You know you could probably find out who the men who arrested Ada were. There's probably a record in some archive. Wouldn't you like to confront them? Force them to acknowledge the consequences of their actions?'

'Once upon a time I would. I wanted to rub it in their faces. But the only purpose it'd serve now is to create hate. They'd hate me for reminding them how abject and cowardly they once were.'

'They might shed tears of remorse. There might be a closure in the act.'

'I once conjured up this image of Hitler. I imagined that he didn't kill himself and that he was kept in a kind of open booth at Auschwitz, like a circus attraction of old times. He had been stripped naked and everyone visiting Auschwitz could let him know what they felt about him. Then I extended the picture. I had hundreds of these booths. There were the SS men who had shot Jews in trenches and in forests, the guards at the camps, the man who owned the company that made the Zyklon B, the men who inserted the canisters into the chutes, the women who had denounced Jews to the secret police and of course all the French gendarmes who took part in the roundup in July 1942. And do you know what I realised? I realised there would be more of my booths than visitors.'

It was now I saw Josh. He was at the wheel of the car and the engine was running. I noticed he had a strange carven expression on his face.

'Fuck you and your charity, old man,' he yelled through the rolled down window as we drew near. He tossed my grandfather's passport out onto the pavement as if it was a burnt piece of toast he was throwing to birds. And then he drove off.

We were both too stunned to say anything. I thought it might be a practical joke; that he would suddenly reappear in the car with a big grin on his face. But it soon became apparent he wasn't going to reappear. The implication seemed to be that my grandfather and I weren't very likeable.

'He must have discovered the money in my rucksack. I had to keep it there. All the lining in my jacket pockets is ripped, you see.' He pulled his pockets inside out to show me the carnage of rips and loose threads. 'At least I've got my passport. And just as well I kept some emergency money in my shoes. In case of muggers.'

'How much money has he taken?'

'I don't know exactly. A lot. I don't use banks. I don't like the way people look at me in banks.'

I realised suddenly I was trapped. On every side, pressing the air out of my lungs, was the prospect of a nightmare train journey.

3 Sister Europe

There were no vacancies at any of the cheap hotels we tried. I never booked anything in advance. That would involve taking for granted intervening time and all its obstacles, something I never managed. And clearly such thoughts didn't ever occur to my grandfather. My grandfather was in a daze. I found it difficult to get his attention. Time, which prevents everything from happening at once, had evidently ceased to exist for him: everything *was* happening all at once. It did me good to assume full responsibility for our predicament. It kept my mind occupied on immediate practicalities. It was me who hunted down hotels, who asked the concierges if there were any free rooms. Darkness soon gathered. We risked spending the night on the streets of Paris. Now and again I was able to marvel at the fact I was in Paris. That I had successfully crossed another frontier. It occurred to me that my phobia brought with it many conditions reminiscent of wartime. The greatly increased proliferation of forbidden zones and frontiers. The enforcement of curfews. The ubiquitous threat of interrogation. And how it stripped one of one's dreams and denied one a freewheeling sensuous kinship with everyday life.

The lights of Paris were ablaze and we were exhausted when we finally found a hotel near Place de la Bastille. My grandfather sat on the bed. He looked drained and absent. He reminded me of an exposed riverbed – the absence of current disclosing a usually hidden intimacy.

'Hadn't you better check how much money you've got hidden?' I said.

He took off his shoes and extracted from his socks two flattened wads of bank notes which he handed to me.

I counted. Eight thousand francs.

There was so much dark nervous energy swirling about in my system that I was relieved when he said he was going to bed. Any close attention on me tonight, I felt, might precipitate an insurrection more anarchic and violent than anything my mind had yet produced. The escape route my imagination in its melodramatic but deadly serious guise offered was to throw myself from the third floor window. This image kept returning. The close proximity of my grandfather in this cramped overly bright room was making me ever more nervous. Therefore I welcomed darkness and the extinguishing of prying eyes. In bed I summoned up an image of Katie dancing in her sherbet pink dress to counter all the uneasiness I felt. If I imagined her watching I felt a little safer, a little braver.

In truth I liked hotel rooms. The absence of anything binding. The ease with which they offered a quick escape. And of course we didn't have any luggage, not even a tooth or hair brush.

My grandfather wanted to stay another day and night in Paris before going to the Vel d'Hiv memorial museum in

Orléans. I welcomed this idea with an inrush of relief. As far as I was concerned I had thirty-six hours of clemency.

'Did you really expect to find your book of spells?' I asked him that night. We were in our separate beds with the raucous skittish noises of Paris at night a presence in the room.

'The past seems fictitious to me tonight,' he said. I waited for him to elaborate but he didn't. I thought of that lost book and all the memories it held and how it was just one of millions of objects in the world loaded with secret history which pass hands until eventually they excite nothing more than mild curiosity or, often, complete apathy. It was like all the sadness and loneliness of life resided in these objects. I realised the moment anything loses its context it becomes a husk. Truth be told I was a bit worried my grandfather, faced with the now irrevocable loss of his and Ada's book of spells, was in the throes of becoming a husk. His mental vigour, his imaginative vitality seemed significantly depleted tonight.

I decided now was the time to mention Katie. I told him she was dancing in Castiglion Fiorentino in Tuscany. Three days from now. 'I'd really like to see her dance,' I said.

'So would I,' he said. 'We'll go there before we go to Venice.'

He hadn't mentioned my phobia of trains. He took it for granted I would still be accompanying him. I was glad of this. I was sick and tired of the prominence it had in my life.

I have a magical memory of Paris that day, especially of sitting in the Jardin du Luxembourg. More than anything I wished I could stop time. The Luxembourg Gardens gave me that illusion for a while. We brought a toothbrush each and some spare underwear. We had matching boxer shorts now. My grandfather insisted on copying me as if I was some kind of authority in the art of shopping. But the ordeal of tomorrow's train journey was like a fin circling the darkening waters of my mind.

There were two reasons for setting off on foot for Gare de Lyon first thing in the morning. Firstly I was always more optimistic at that time of day and secondly I reasoned the train would be less full. The streets of Paris had an almost transparent quality as if washed in watered ink. That illusion early morning often gives of returning you to a childhood where everything might be begun from scratch was there as part of my response to the dawning of a new day but over-ruled by all the tension I was carrying in my body. I felt light on my feet, the ground seemed to tilt and sway beneath me, as if I had just stepped off a merry go round.

My heart spent too much time every day beating too fast. Unlike most habits fear is not one you ever get used to. The demands it makes on the strength of your root system never diminish. The body never tires of producing fear as if it's one of its favourite occupations. I lit another cigarette and reminded myself I was not about to be herded onto a cattle train destined for a crematoria.

On the train I told my grandfather not to sit opposite me. I felt I might be able to go through with this as long as no one sat facing me. When the engine started my stomach lurched. For a moment my instinct was to dash to the door and fling it open before the train started moving.

Every time the train stopped at a station my heart thumped with the fear someone was going to sit down opposite me.

My grandfather had fallen asleep. I can't say I envied him his oblivion because he still seemed to me subdued and more physically vulnerable than I had ever known him.

After half an hour I began to relax. My mind began to allow me natural responses to my situation. I was plugged into my Walkman. Songs carry memories almost as reliably and poignantly as smells. My favourite songs all belonged to the time before my expulsion from Paradise – the world where I was able to take simple things for granted. The innocence of my ignorance of how much terror and distortion my mind was capable of throwing at me. I didn't particularly love my childhood; there wasn't much there that provided me with sustenance or reassurance. The time of my relationship with Katie had become my childhood. It thrilled me how much vitality there still was hoarded in all these old songs. They had never sounded so uplifting, so eloquent in expressing the importance of courage in life.

In the museum, not being Jewish, I felt a bit of a fraud. I don't know why since it obviously wasn't mandatory to be Jewish. But I felt on the wrong side of the fence. It had never once in my life occurred to me to wonder if someone was Jewish. It had less relevance to me than if they owned a cat or not. Obviously some of the faces I saw in the photographs were more likeable than others. One or two I felt guilty for not liking. I suppose I can just about imagine why men who made a song and dance of being Jewish, who flaunted their difference, attracted hostility. The men with the sidelocks and the beards and the black hats and black robes. They often looked like wizards. People who held sheepishly to a high level of social conformity as a moral fulcrum and judged by appearances wouldn't have liked that. I had first hand of experience of the hostility you incur when you cross convention's boundaries. From the age of sixteen, inspired by David Bowie, I wore make up out into the world every day. Hostility was something you had to accept if you chose to stand out in a crowd. It's not right of course but sadly it seems a fact of life.

I wasn't sure any of the faces in the photographs wanted my sympathy. I was uncomfortable meeting eyes. The lonely impotence they forced me to own. Some, often those caught by a professional photographer, looked at me with a polite but hounded cast to their features. Others seemed gifted with an eerie clairvoyance as if they sensed what awaited them. It was the faces alight with an eagerness for the next moment which caused me the most distress. Often these were the children. In every face I thought I perceived an appeal no one would ever meet. A lifetime of denied expectation arrested in a single expression. They were the faces of people with all their promise ended. The feeling of destiny produced by the images was overwhelming. The absolute minimum of control these people had in their lives, the paltry resources they had to survive.

I didn't see the moment my grandfather caught sight of Ada's photograph on the wall. I had understood he needed to be alone and I made a point of keeping my distance. But I knew something momentous had happened when I saw him walking towards me. He had an air of walking through obstacles as ghosts are said to do. He was looking down at the ground as though at the splash and spillage of the contents of a bottle he had let slip through his hands. He took me by the arm and guided me along the marbled aisle of black and white photographs. The photograph was down close to the ground and I had to sit on the floor. Ada was standing by her mother who, sitting in an armchair, was sowing a button onto a shirt laid out in her lap. She perhaps was the best example of all of a face radiant with eagerness for the next moment. Ada, locked into another moment of time, wearing her death-mask. I was surprised when tears welled up behind my eyes.

We returned to Paris that same day. I wasn't so nervous this time. I'm reluctant to believe in good news and choose not to dwell on it for more than a moment. Take it too much to heart and it invariably has to be paid for with a hangover. So I didn't for one moment believe my affliction was now a thing of the past. There would be no miracle cures. But I felt now that I might have the resources to fight it. Today my grandfather's emotion took precedence over my own. He was shaken up and I felt protective of him. He made me forget myself, sometimes the most precious gift one person can give another.

'I was expecting her to reproach me,' my grandfather said. He had been staring out of the window, gnawing his thumb-nail. He was sitting opposite me.

'But she didn't?'

'No. At first I didn't really recognise her in that photo. It was like she was spurning me as I had spurned her that afternoon on the quay. Then I got out my magnifying glass.' He began fishing in the lining of his jacket and, after a strug-gle, produced the glass to show me. 'When I looked at her through this she moved for a split second. Or she appeared to. It was like she left the imprisoning frame. Then I had her face as I remember it returned to me. I remembered she sang a lot. Or hummed. I remembered she cuffed me and laughed when she disagreed with me. And I remembered the way her mother said my name. She always called me Massimiliano. Everyone else called me Max. I can't remember how Ada said my name. I did though catch the faintest echo of her voice. I remembered how the sound of her voice made me instantaneously happy. It's extraordinary how much of someone you can find and hold onto in the sound of their voice.'

I nodded, an inept response because I wanted to hug him, a new impulse in me.

'One thing, you mustn't think I think obsessively of Ada. When I do think of her she comes mostly of her own accord and it lasts no more than a minute. But in that minute I'm more alive, more keenly responsive to the wondrous and devastating heartbeat of life. If I forced myself to think about her often this wouldn't be true. Memories are like the heart; you mustn't ask too much of them. Just let them get on quietly with their schooling.'

He held his hand to his heart. I realised I had seen him perform this gesture more than once over the past two days but was only now registering it.

4 Station to Station

Few things have ever tasted better than the baguette I ate sitting beside my grandfather on the pavement outside the Gare de Lyon. The sun was setting over the Parisian rooftops. I was excited now, instead of dry-mouthed with dread. For once my mind was loading the appropriate data.

'We're about to enter your narrative now,' my grandfather said.

The night train to Florence, for all its seediness, possessed an exotic quality for me. I felt a child's sense of wonder and excitement that I would be climbing a ladder to sleep on a bed which would accompany me across a continent. And no one would be spying on me. I would be immured with my music within a secret nest. I could hardly believe this was my third train in one day. This all happened in the good old days when you could still buy a ticket on the train; when you didn't have to book everything in your life in advance.

We shared the couchette with an elderly French couple and a lone young black man from Somalia. My grandfather talked to them all in French. He told me the boy was a dancer. Five hours later he was to be taken off the train by border police who came into our compartment at two in the morning when we were all lying in our bunks in the dark under a scratchy blanket. My grandfather was indignant on the boy's behalf and argued with the gun-carrying Italian police in French. His hostility towards these border guards, in constant crescendo, was plain as day even if expressed in a language I didn't understand. I was caught in two minds. On the one hand I liked the boy; he had a smile which made his eyes shine and which, I felt, showed him to have a kind and generous heart. On the other hand I didn't like the hostile attention my grandfather was drawing to us and wished he would stay silent. I knew he was thinking of the men who had arrested Ada and couldn't stem his anger. He mentioned Mussolini's name at one point. For a moment I thought he was going to perform the fascist salute. Instead I saw him place his hand on his heart and grimace. The border guards eventually turned their attention to me. They didn't like me much either and wanted to search my bag and grew still more suspicious when my grandfather told them I didn't have a bag.

'What was all that about?' I asked when they had gone and the train was rocking through the Italian night.

'They said he was carrying a forged passport.'

'In that case...'

'I didn't like the way they treated him. In some men's minds black skin is the equivalent of the yellow star. They think it gives them the right to withhold all respect, to spit in someone's face.'

I went out into the corridor to smoke a cigarette. All the blinds of the other compartments were drawn. The earthy smell of a new day dawning thieved in through the open windows. There was a sense of a lurking epiphany in the moment. But I was too troubled to receive it. The scene with the border police had revealed something about myself I didn't like. A tendency to put my own interests first, to fake oblivion in the face of the persecution of others. I suspected I would have offered no resistance during the war, no help to those in peril; that I might have been one of the Nazi puppets my grandfather spoke of.

We spent the morning in Florence. My grandfather noticed a plaque in Piazza Santa Maria Novella commemorating the Jews transported from a prison there to the death camps. That plaque seemed to explain why the wide square with its emerald green grass and loggia and coloured marble basilica, which should have been uplifting, had instead an oppressive unclean fume about it, an atmosphere that rasped over the skin like the lick of a cat's tongue. It seemed proof that places retain some memory of what happened there.

It was early evening, after yet another train journey, when we walked from the station up to the hilltop town of Castiglion Fiorentino. Our shadows sometimes preceded us, sometimes followed in our wake. My grandfather complained of a pain in his chest. We weren't drinking enough water. Come to think of it we weren't drinking any water. We were both out of breath when we reached the summit. The summer heat clothed our bodies. The air smelt of scorched dust and crushed herbs. Honeyed light, broken by russet-tiled rooftops, was a shimmer over the old stones and made them look ghostly. The grain of wooden doors was visible underneath the paint. The past everywhere was an intimate presence.

At least tonight the high tide swill of agitation I now knew every day of my life was a natural response to the situation at hand. A nervousness most would feel in my position. I was about to see Katie for the first time since the abortion. It occurred to me that the last time we spent a night together I was a glamorous figure on the cusp of stardom; now I was a damaged nobody without prospects. My former band had toured America, Japan and the whole of Europe; they had appeared on Top of the Pops, The Old Grey Whistle Test and various other TV programmes around the world. They were all now recognised in the street; they had money to burn; I was claiming unemployment benefit and sharing a room in a half-way house with a stranger.

5 Gentle Moon

The performance was to be staged out in the open air, in a sloping piazza flanked by elegant medieval and renaissance buildings. I had to position myself at the end of the scrum of plastic seats, removed from the press of humanity. I needed to feel I had a quick escape route if my head betrayed me.

There was a high brick wall on the stage. The lights dimmed. All attention focused on the wall. Suddenly it toppled over. A slender woman in a shapeless lilac dress clambered over the fallen stones. She appeared distressed and exposed like a woman in times of conflict. A song started up, thin and crackling like something played on a wartime gramophone.

The music became an earthy impassioned chant, an ethnic drumbeat snaking down into the loins like the pulse of beating blood in the dark. And there was Katie, in a green dress, her long black hair loose. She danced on the spot as if constrained within a tiny circle. There was a shimmy of the hips, an elegant little skip, a windmill motion of the arm, suppliant and then sleeping gestures of the hands, a shuffling of the feet. The movements were almost everyday enactments of the body but with mesmerising secret quirks. It was as if she was ushering a liquid current through her body as she danced. I found myself shaping her movements inside my own body without any conscious effort on my part. All my muscles straining with hers. The imaginative identification I achieved was exhilarating. I felt I was moving in unison with Katie in some realm just outside myself. As if I was wearing her movements like clothes. For a moment I thought about her clothes. Clothes that had once been tangled with my own on the moonlit floor of her bedroom. I imagined I had access to all the clothes she had ever worn when she was with me, that I could hold them in my hands, run my fingers over them, press them to my face. There's something moving about the memory of the clothes of a cherished friend, an example of the transfiguring nature of memory. At the time I can't ever remember being bewitched by any article of clothing Katie wore. Some things of course suited her better than others. But essentially they were just coloured pieces of cloth. After I lost her they became tokens of her bewitching power to grant wishes; they took on the mystery of sacred relics.

It occurred to me that dance is probably the most faithful dramatisation of the act of memory. Every image alive with a haunting clarity and then vanishing almost as soon as it appears, leaving in its wake an elusive imprint of itself. Most art forms seek to transcend time; dance uses time as its medium.

There was something heartbreaking about the sight of Katie's bare feet, how intimately known to me they once were and now how remote and inaccessible. I was reminded of her stealing the sheet from our bed, drawing it around her naked body and tramping off to the kitchen with a backward smiling glance at me lying naked and exposed on the mattress. Her footprints a fleeting imprint on the carpet like tracks on dew.

When the performance ended my grandfather told me he was tired and wasn't feeling so good. He went back to the hotel. I remained in the piazza while men collected the plastic chairs and stacked them under a loggia. A long time passed before Katie eventually appeared from the makeshift dressing room in the backstage area. I watched her receive the congratulations of a group of people she seemed to know. And then she saw me across the ghost light of the now deserted piazza. Her first reaction was shock, as if she thought I was stalking her. Then she smiled, but to herself, not to me. Then she carried on talking to her friends. I understood she wasn't going to come over and talk to me. Oddly, I was relieved. My heart stopped thumping. I was free to enjoy the moment. It was enough that she had seen me there. By not coming over she proved to me how well she knew me. Why trivialise the moment with a merry go round of chit chat? Enact a trite parody of our former intimacy. There had been times in the past when we talked as if we only had until sunrise to say everything we needed to say to each other. I felt she understood that there had been nothing acquisitive in the impulse that had brought me here to see her dance. But the act of our eyes meeting over this hilltop Italian piazza had, I felt, revived everything that was good and fortifying in our relationship, made it ongoing. Until now any good I had done Katie was no longer an enlivening resource within either of us; it was this I wanted to change. I wanted her to be able to think of me without anger. I wanted her to realise it might in the future be a comfort to her that I was out in the world someplace. As I knew it would always be a comfort to me that she was out in the world somewhere.

I was sad though that she hadn't met my grandfather. I had been embarrassed by my parents when introducing them to Katie. Especially my mother and her slavish conformity to convention. She was like someone who never comes up to the surface. It was as if all her soil had been overlaid with unseeded astro turf. My mother was incapable of intimacy and that's why I often felt ashamed of her.

Later, in bed in the hotel room, I saw Katie dance again, with a startling fragmented vividness, except she was tiny, as though she were dancing in the palm of my hand. The picture was like something torn out of the dark by the beam of a torch. Move the torch and it ceased to exist.

The next day we caught another train to Florence and yet another to Venice. I was anxious again and angry that I was still anxious. I noticed my grandfather's movements had become more laboured in the last couple of days. Sometimes every physical effort on his part reminded me of the double grinding of a key in a rusted lock. I also saw he wrapped his feet around the legs of chairs or braced his stomach against counters as if his body needed the stability of some form of rail to hold onto.

Walking out of the station of Santa Lucia and beholding the Grand Canal felt like stepping onto a stage and bowing to thundering applause. I stood watching the water buses arrive and leave, the gondoliers ease their boats towards the open sea. I felt momentarily cleansed of all detritus, as if I myself had overcome all the obstacles necessary for the creation of everything I saw and now took to heart. Then my grandfather lurched forward with his hand pressed to his heart. The movement was shocking in its abruptness. I thought for a moment he was going to perform one of his dances. As if the grimace on his face and the sudden seizure of his shoulders was part of the performance. It wasn't. My grandfather was having a heart attack.

6 For the Love of Life

It struck me as incongruous that there was a hospital in Venice. My first impression of Venice was that it might be hard to make anything happen there. Everything seemed to have already happened. Venice seemed like a kind of exalted remembering. And yet something had happened here. My grandfather had had a heart attack.

I called my mother. Not even the death of her father brought her up to the surface. If anything it compelled her to burrow down deeper in her emotional bunker. More difficult to register for her than his death seemed the fact that I had accompanied my grandfather to Venice. She kept telling me she didn't understand. She made it sound as if we had betrayed her in some way. While sitting by the Grand Canal that night I wondered if my mother had spent her life insulating herself from what she perceived as the mental instability of my grandfather, as if it might be contagious. It seemed as though she had dumped all his baggage on my doorstep. While staring out at all the coloured lights on the water I felt how glad I was of all this baggage.

The address of the woman my grandfather was supposed to meet was in his jacket pocket. He had fastened it with a safety pin so it didn't disappear into the torn lining. I still couldn't own the fact of his death. He had died in the ambulance, which was a boat. He had died on the Grand Canal. In the city where he had been born. His life had followed the circumference of a perfect circle. I wondered without arriving at any kind of answer what this meant.

I wasn't prepared for how upset the woman would be when I explained what had happened to my grandfather. It was more out of a sense of duty that I visited her than with any expectation of appeasing my grief. She was an elderly woman and like my grandfather her bones caught the eye more than her skin. She was wearing tapered black slacks and a silk blouse the same shade of blue as the Chelsea kit which had so enamoured me as a child. She told me to call her Francesca.

'I was your grandfather's half-sister. His father was my father. Which I suppose makes me your great aunt.'

So she was the daughter of the man who had raped my grandfather's mother. Obviously I couldn't voice my astonishment aloud. For a moment I felt myself aglow with an explosive secret. I did my best to hide my discomfort from her.

'That's his mother up there on the wall,' she said. 'My father painted it.'

Now it was confusion I sought to hide from her. I looked up at the framed painting. It made me momentary angry how close my grandfather had come to seeing again the image he carried around with him as a small boy. I'm no expert on painting but it seemed very accomplished to me.

'There are two of his paintings in the Peggy Guggenheim museum. I'll take you to see them. My father did all he could to find your grandfather after the war. Shall we call him Max rather than *your grandfather*? That's what I'm accustomed to calling him. My father wrote to the woman who brought Max up but she didn't reply. Camille, her name was. My father survived Mauthausen concentration camp. He was very sick for years afterwards. By the time he was able to travel to Paris Max had disappeared without trace as had the couple who brought him up. What was he like, my brother?'

I said he was a wonderful man and endeavoured to elaborate but my eulogy sounded trite and formulaic. I didn't have my grandfather's gift of the gab. In fact this memoir was probably born out of the deeply felt inadequacy of my reply to her question.

'When Elisa found out she was pregnant her first thought was to abort the child. She was only twenty years old. But apparently the place she went to was so filthy that she took to her heels. You, like Max, therefore owe your existence to poor health and safety measures. Makes you think, doesn't it? My father and Elisa fell out over her decision to give away the baby. They split up.'

'So your father and Elisa were lovers?'

'Childhood sweethearts. They had been together since the age of sixteen.'

'My grandfather was told Elisa didn't know the father.'

'That doesn't surprise me. My father never knew what excuse Elisa gave Camille for not being able to keep the child. He suspected it was a pack of lies. She was no doubt secretly ashamed of the real reason which was that her heart was set on being a dancer. She was determined to study modern dance with a dancer called Martha Graham in America. Camille was probably in love with Elisa. That's what my father thought. Even though she was older she was like Elisa's personal slave. Would do anything Elisa asked of her. I can't remember, if I ever knew, how they knew each other. Elisa worked at a hotel while studying dance but to earn extra money for the trip to America she worked as an undercover agent for OVRA, Mussolini's secret police. One or two students at the university were arrested and sent into exile as a result of her reports. Suspicions about her began to circulate. My father confronted her. He was still in love with her. But he said he could no longer get through to her. That he no longer recognised her. Then, three weeks before she was to depart for America, a group of excited children ran at her and she stumbled down some steps and broke a bone in her foot. She came to think of it as a punishment from God for abandoning her child. She quit working for Mussolini's secret police and her and my father got back together. They decided to fetch the child from Paris. Elisa caught the train to Paris. Except OVRA agents hauled her off at the border. They were suspicious she had turned. That she was going to Paris to meet exiled Italian communists there. Then of course the war began. My father was Jewish so he wasn't wanted in the army. He was forced into work details, doing menial work. My father went into hiding when the Nazis occupied the country. Late in 1943 Elisa was concealing a Jewish family in her apartment. They were about to be taken to a monastery in the Veneto when they were arrested and deported. Word went round that Elisa had betrayed them and received the reward. Her past caught up with her. My father knew this wasn't true. She loved the little boy as if he was her own, which she was probably pretending he was. He was about the same age as Max. My father was eventually arrested, not as a Jew but as a partisan. Elisa, it's believed, was executed as a traitor at the end of the war. Her body was fished out of a canal. By the time my father returned from all the post-war transit camps she had long since been buried.'

'I wish my grandfather, Max, could have heard all of this. He's died thinking his mother was a heartless monster.'

'We've got a couple of photos of her. I'll go and get them out.'

The high-ceilinged room was full of claw-footed furniture and houseplants. A beautiful silver nine branched candelabrum on a sideboard stood out. I recognised it as a Jewish ceremonial artefact but did not then know its name or purpose.

I studied the painting for a while. My great grandmother preserved in oils and varnishes. Thanks to her, I realised, or, more precisely, her choice of lover, I had some Jewish blood in my body. The discovery was exciting. All of a sudden I was extended over a larger part of the world's map, as if the reach of my empire had grown. This, I thought, was what empire should mean. Not the occupation of nations by military force but an occupation of spirit, a recognition of the many branched interacting veins of heritage. I thought back to the wall of the photographs at the Holocaust memorial when I had felt like an outsider, standing on the wrong side of the fence so to speak. How little I had known then. I realised too my grandfather and Ada had had even more in common than he thought. That, legally, he too should have worn the yellow star on his left breast. And that maybe his mother had saved his life by giving him away. It was another source of regret that he hadn't known this.

I walked over to the second floor window which looked down on a canal. Two moored gondolas creaked as they were buffeted gently by the tide. Seaweed washed up on the steps was fretted by the sluggish rise and fall of the water. The palazzo opposite with its mullioned and arched windows and red geraniums was reflected as vividly in the water as it appeared before my eyes. A couple passed by and I watched them walk upside down in the liquid green world beneath the water. I thought enviously of what a lovely place to live this must be. And there were no trains or tubes in Venice. Then I felt guilty, as if I was disrespecting the death of my grandfather by thinking ahead.

Women in photos from bygone decades, those before the 1950s I mean, rarely appear attractive to me. There often seems something overly fussy about them, as if they are wearing a mask of prim innocence. The living pulse seems faint, an inner life deeply submerged. It's like women, whether twenty or eighty years old, became more outwardly beautiful the more of themselves they were able to dramatise to the world. Elisa wasn't beautiful in my eyes. She didn't look fussy though. She looked like she loved to come up to the surface.

A buzzer sounded. The echoing brutality of it startled me.

'That will be my daughter and granddaughter,' said Francesca. A woman and a little girl entered the drawing room. The little girl had an elfin face and long dark hair which she kept flicking at.

'Now then, I'm not sure I can work this out,' said Francesca. 'Avira, let's say this young man is your uncle. His name is Mark. Marco, like the piazza. Why don't you tell Mark one of your stories?'

The little girl looked doubtful. She hid her face behind her hands and then pressed her face into her mother's midriff.

'Go on,' said her mother. 'He won't bite. Tell him the story you told me last night.'

'I'd love to hear one of your stories,' I said.

She looked up at me shyly, interrogatively. Her steady, seemingly mindreading gaze held me in its orbit. It was like she wasn't going to stop looking at me until she reassured herself of something crucial. For a moment I felt I was on trial and that it was immensely important I was found innocent. 'Okay,' she said. She stepped away from her mother and braced herself. 'This is a story about love. Far far in the distance, three thousand fifty billion hundred years ago, that's how love was created,' she said. She twisted and cavorted as she spoke, throwing her arms about and making extravagant gestures with her hands as if trying to lift her words up into the air. 'Love was created before the universe made the land. Everything was dark and there was no god. Love was the first thing that ever existed. First there was just plain black, no god, no nothing. There was just love, rising above. The first part of your love goes to your mother. Then your father. He has to wait. Because you're connected to your mother. You're in your mummy's tummy. Love is the big universe we can't see. It goes way way out there. When we go to death love goes with us and that's how everyone gets born again. Because there isn't only one of us. When people can't feel love they are like ants who think the world is no bigger than the garden path where they live. They have a tiny tiny world and they follow the ant in front. And that's a little story about love.'

'Avira, you're so right about ants,' I said. 'I've never understood why they receive so much praise. Slaves to routine is what they are. Give me butterflies any day.'

She walked over to me and took hold of my hand and leant her weight against me. I almost recoiled from the surge of wellbeing her warmth and weight flooded into me. It was probably the loveliest compliment I had ever received. I realised while all her vulnerability made itself felt in the press of her hand that had Katie not had an abortion I would now have a child of roughly her age. Perhaps a gorgeous little girl, like Avira. I understood the final decision lay with Katie and I understood why she had made the decision but I didn't see why I wasn't allowed to feel some sadness for the lost child. My mistake had been to not keep the sadness a secret.

Then I thought of Ada. I realised I had learned her face by heart. The face on which all her promise ended. I animated my image of her with all Avira's vitality and power to enchant and pictured her being ushered by grown men along the path towards the gas chambers. Only, I realised, the contingencies of time had saved the beautiful girl holding my hand from the same fate.

Then I wished Avira was holding my grandfather's hand instead of mine.

'You'll stay for supper?'

I nodded.

At least for a while I didn't have to ask myself how I was going to get home.

Acknowledgements

For inspiration, sustenance and feedback, thanks to:

Charles Cecil, Freddie de Rougemont, Georgiana Calthorpe, Emily Pennock, VJ Keegan, Rupert Alexander, Vanessa Garwood, Antonia Barclay, Justin Sparrow, Anna von Kanitz, Jessica St. James, Lucy Corbett, Tom Lumley, Talitha Stevenson, Charlie Warde, Paola Rosà, Gina Monaco, Tim Binding, Alex Preston, Judith Kinghorn, Annabel Merullo, Charlie Campbell, Hamid Khanbhai, Christabel Brudnell-Bruce, Charlotte Raymond, David Flusfeder, Tim Atkins, Tiarnan McCarthy, Sarah Haybittle, Chiara De Cabarrus, Lisa Andris, Kim Macconnell, Rachel Webster, Stuart Bridgeman, Linda Fleischman, Hugo Wilson, Eloise Anson, Caroline Scott, Marc Dalessio, Paolo Cristellotti, Mark Roberts, Richard Burton, Katie St. George, Charlotte Cecil, Josephine Rea, Bill Liesegang, Ebba Heuman, Cristina Zamagni.